Miracle on
Chance Avenue

MIRACLE ON CHANCE AVENUE

A Love on Chance Avenue Romance

JANE PORTER

TULE
PUBLISHING

DEDICATION

For all the wonderful, amazing readers who have taken
Marietta, Montana into your hearts. This one is for you!

PROLOGUE

S HE WAS BACK.

It had been almost a month since Rory Douglas had last seen her, so long that he'd almost stopped looking for her every night. But now she was back in the stands, this time in Clovis, California, over halfway across the country from the last time he'd spotted her in Santa Fe, and before Santa Fe, it had been Nashville.

She was even more beautiful tonight, her brilliant copper red hair in a loose side braid, the expression in her brown eyes somber as she watched Kane Wilder dash out of the ring after his electrifying ride.

Rory's pulse quickened when she turned her head and looked at him, finding him in his chute. Their gazes locked, and Rory didn't look away, wanting her to know he saw her, and remembered her. Each time, every time. The first time he'd spotted her in the stands had been two and a half years ago in Coeur d'Alene, Idaho. It wasn't a big stadium, and she'd been so beautiful she seemed to glow with light and life. She'd seemed familiar, too, but he wasn't sure why.

Two and a half years later he still didn't know anything

about her, and yet his gut told him she was there for him, that her appearances at the various tour events these past few years had always been for him.

Or maybe he just wanted her to be there for him.

Maybe his ego needed to believe that beautiful, young things were still attracted to him, despite the fact that he was the oldest man on the American Extreme Bull Rider Tour, earning Rory the nickname Gramps from the other guys.

Rory didn't mind the nickname. At thirty-eight he *was* too old to still be competing, and twice the age of the youngest athletes. But competing kept him on the road, and busy, and too tired and sore to think of anything but getting through the next day. He liked the guys on tour, too. Over the years they'd become his family, a tough, practical, uncomplaining family, which suited him just fine because his real family was far more complicated, which was another way of saying painful, and at times, more bitter than sweet.

Every night after Rory chalked his rope, taped up his hands, and stretched, he'd say a prayer as he settled onto the back of his bull.

He didn't ask God to keep him safe. He didn't ask for anything for himself, but rather he prayed that the good Lord would keep His hand over his sister McKenna's head. He prayed that his brother Quinn would one day find a good woman and have a family. And then he'd pray that both of them would know peace after he was gone.

But tonight, just as he was about to climb into the chute,

he'd felt that pull, that now familiar, taut, electric tension that told him she was there, the tension that made him lift his gaze and search the stands until he found her.

His mystery woman, a woman he'd come to think of as his angel.

Rory lowered his weight onto Hammerfall's back and tightened the rope, wrapping it tightly around his hand as calm and resolve settled into his bones. He wouldn't die tonight, not with her here in the stands. It wouldn't be fair. It wasn't the way he wanted to be remembered.

Attention now fixed between the bull's massive shoulders, Rory nodded his head, indicating he was good to go. And then the chute opened, and Hammerfall charged into the ring, bucking and twisting, and Rory settled back into the pocket, or what he hoped would be the pocket, but inexplicably Hammerfall gyrated the opposite direction, flinging Rory forward while the bull threw his head back. Rory knew a split second before the impact that it wasn't going to be good, and he found himself praying just before all went black.

Give me a chance, Lord.

CHAPTER ONE

THE WORST PART about being the newest employee was that you had the least amount of seniority, which was why Sadie Mann was standing outside a tiny historic stable turned into stylish small house at the end of Farrell Avenue, shivering in the snow, waiting for the renter to show and pick up the keys at nine thirty at night.

She didn't mind meeting the guest who'd booked the property as her house wasn't far and Marietta had virtually no crime, but it was ridiculously cold, and she'd been waiting an awfully long time. There were so many projects she could be working on right now, commissions she still needed to get in the mail if they were to reach her customers before Christmas.

But she'd manage it, she would, she told herself, hunching her shoulders against yet another blast of cold air, the wind as much a part of Marietta as the famed Copper Mountain peak standing sentry behind the town's historic courthouse.

Yes, it might mean missing the Marietta Stroll tomorrow night, something she'd never missed before, not even when she was flying with Big Sky Air, as it was her annual tradition with her mom, but Mom was gone, having passed away suddenly in September and Sadie had accepted that things were different. She was different. She'd given up her fantasies and daydreams and had turned over a new leaf. Her goal was to be strong, self-sufficient, and practical. And practical was the most challenging of the three.

Being practical had become her mantra since Rory was hurt, and then came her mom's death, and being practical took on a whole new meaning. With her mom gone, Sadie realized just how foolish she'd been, chasing impossible dreams all these years, with Rory the biggest dream of all.

Getting over Rory wasn't proving to be easy. Maybe it was because the last time she saw him was at the hospital in Clovis and he'd been a bear, out of his mind with pain, but at least he was alive.

She'd gone to the hospital to make sure he was breathing. She'd gone to make sure he'd survive.

But looking at his poor, battered body, with all those bandages and tubes and tape, she didn't feel sorry for him, she felt angry. He was doing this to himself. He wanted out. He didn't care about living.

That was why she'd wanted to have his baby. It was why she'd shown up at the arenas for over two years. She wasn't there to watch him ride. She was there to figure out how to ask him to sleep with her. But every time she saw him, her courage deserted her. *How did you ask a man like Rory to get you pregnant?*

How did you say, *"Hey, I've loved you since I was thirteen and I've spent my life waiting for you, and loving you from afar, and if I can't have you, maybe I could just have a piece of you…"*

Of course, you didn't say it because it was crazy, and yet it hadn't stopped Sadie from dreaming and praying.

But then when her mom died, Sadie's world collapsed, and she'd taken an indefinite leave of absence from the airline while she tried to come to terms with who she was, and where she was at thirty-five, and that was alone, most singularly alone. Sadie also knew she had no one but herself to blame as she'd spent her life waiting for someone, and something, that would never happen.

But that was going to change.

She'd already changed.

She'd given up working for the airline to make a new life for herself in Marietta, a life that was stable, and grounded, a life that meant she was putting herself first and only dating nice, local, emotionally available men. She wouldn't let herself think of these nice emotionally available men as boring, either. And she most definitely wouldn't let herself compare them to Rory. It wasn't fair to them, or her.

But, even more significantly, she was moving forward in her desire to be a mom. She didn't have to have Rory's baby to be a mother. The world was filled with men, and fertility clinics, and sperm donors. She didn't need to be married to be a mom. She didn't need to wait. She had a home and savings, and she wasn't getting any younger. If she wanted to have children, she needed to do it now, while she could conceive.

That was why she was working so hard, juggling her online shabby chic business, *The Montana Rose*, with her job at Marietta Properties, along with the occasional babysitting/dog sitting/housesitting job. The plan was to sock away as much money as she could right now, so she could afford to take some time off when the baby came.

Lights shone in the distance and an old white pickup truck came into view. Sadie watched as the truck slowed and parked next to the curb. The lights turned off, and the driver door swung open. Her heart did a hard, uncomfortable thump as a tall man in a sheepskin coat approached, boots and cane crunching snow, his black felt cowboy hat drawn low on his brow.

Her heart did another hard thump, and she felt a frisson of pleasure followed by a streak of pain.

It couldn't be... it couldn't...

And yet she recognized that square jaw with just a hint of golden brow bristle and she knew that black felt hat, too. The limp, and the cane, those were new, but the rest was achingly familiar.

Rory Douglas.

There weren't many street lights in this part of town, and the small porch lights framing the doors of the old stable created two small pools of light that did little to illuminate the shoveled sidewalk or the man.

"Sorry I've kept you waiting," he said, his voice deep, hard, as hard as his carved jaw.

She knew that voice, too, along with that firm chin and beautiful mouth that had never once kissed her, but she'd fantasized plenty. "Not a problem," she answered huskily, legs feeling weak.

He stopped in front of her, head lifting a fraction, his narrowed gaze settling on her face. Recognition dawned. "If it isn't the mystery girl from the Extreme Tour."

Her chest squeezed closed. "Hello, Rory."

"Now surely this can't be a coincidence."

"Actually, it is. I was told to meet Ron Douglas. Either it was a typo, or you're using another name these days."

"Only when I'm back in Marietta."

"Why?"

"Easier." His head tipped, his gaze burning into her. He studied her for a long, uncomfortable minute. "It was you at St. Agnes in Fresno, wasn't it?" he said finally.

"What are you talking about?"

"You came to the hospital. I think I was an ass. Chased you away."

She couldn't believe he remembered. He'd been so out of it, almost incoherent with pain.

"I owe you an apology."

"You don't."

"I said things I shouldn't have."

"It's fine," she said finally, her insides on fire because it was.

She hadn't minded that he'd been short-tempered. She hadn't minded his pain. What she'd objected to was the bull stomping on his hip and driving his head and horns into Rory's chest.

That was what she minded.

"You went to get the nurse," he added quietly, "and you never came back."

She struggled to smile, a professional smile, the kind she'd give clients who walked into the real estate office enquiring about a listing. "You didn't need me there."

"I don't know about that, darlin'."

Part of her burned, while another part of her raged.

It was too late.

All of this was too damn late.

Face hot, body cold, Sadie reached into her coat pocket for the keys, not wanting to do this with him, not now. Possibly not ever. Watching him nearly die in front of her had changed her, but she'd finally woken up, thank God.

She flashed him another tight, hard smile. "I'm supposed to let you in, show you around, and answer any questions you might have about Marietta, but since you're from here, I can't imagine you'll have many questions."

"I do have one."

Her gaze met his.

"Why did you show up to all those tour events and never come talk to me?"

A fresh wave of heartache and heat surged through her, the heat knotting in her chest while the rest of her remained frozen. "It doesn't matter anymore."

"It does to me."

She squared her shoulders, lifted her chin. "I liked to make sure you were okay."

"I kept waiting for you to come back."

"You shouldn't have returned to the circuit."

"Now you sound like my sister."

"She loves you. Just like everyone else in this town—" Sadie broke off, eyes stinging, a lump filling her throat, making it impossible to finish her thought. But then, he didn't need her to finish anyway. He knew all this and more. The last thing any of them needed was her trying to insert herself into his life when she couldn't even manage her own.

Turning to the door, she blinked back tears she'd never let him see. Crazy to think she'd been standing here waiting for him. How impossible, how implausible to be back here in Marietta waiting for Rory Douglas?

And just when she'd finally given him up, he appeared.

It wasn't fair, but then, life wasn't supposed to be fair. Life was just life, and capricious as all heck.

"Let's get you inside," she said, trying to slide the key into the deadbolt. "It should be warm inside. I turned the heater on when I first got here. It's an efficient heater and a small space, but I think you'll like it. You're a little far to walk downtown from here, but there is a small convenience store and liquor store just a block over." She was babbling, but she couldn't help it.

When she'd left the Fresno hospital, she'd been hurt, and confused, but she hadn't planned on leaving him behind. But weeks later her mother died and then her world came crashing in, and Sadie realized it was time to stop chasing false dreams. She wasn't a girl anymore. She was thirty-five and single and absolutely alone, and she'd always be alone if she didn't find someone real, and someone dependable, to love.

Only Rory had been part of her heart so long that it'd hurt to let him go. It'd hollowed what was left of her heart, and she knew she had no one to blame but herself.

"Need a hand?" he asked quietly.

She shook her head, not trusting herself to speak. He wasn't supposed to be here. He didn't return to Marietta. McKenna said he avoided his hometown at all costs. And yet he stood tall and solid just behind her, his thick sheepskin accenting his broad shoulders and the width of his muscular chest.

RORY STOOD SILENTLY as he watched Sadie struggle with the key. Her hand was trembling, and he wasn't sure if she was nervous or simply cold. She'd been waiting for over forty minutes. She had to be frozen through. He'd tried calling to say that he'd be late, due to an accident outside of Billings that had shut all traffic down, but his call to Marietta Properties had gone straight to voicemail.

"Have you worked for Marietta Properties long?" he asked, as she tried a different key.

"Just since the end of September," she answered, shooting him a swift glance over her shoulder. Even in a thick puffy coat with a gray knit cap on her head, she looked heart-stoppingly pretty. "And I'm not sure why the lock is sticking. It opened right up before. Not sure what I'm doing wrong."

"I'm happy to try," he said easily, aware as she went back to the first key.

She was becoming increasingly flustered, but there was no hurry. He was happy just to look at her. When she'd walked out of his hospital room in Fresno, he knew he'd see her again, his gut told him he'd see her, but it'd never crossed his mind that he'd find her in Marietta.

As far as he knew, there were no angels in Marietta. All the angels around here had already gone to heaven.

"It's my job to do this," she muttered, trying the first key again. "How difficult can it be to unlock a door?"

"You said you did it before."

She threw him a swift glance, frustration and a nameless emotion darkening her eyes. "Exactly!" And then with a shake of her head, she turned to face him, her long ponytail sliding across her shoulder in a bright gleam of copper. "Okay. I'll give you a shot before we both freeze to death."

She handed him the small key ring, her fingers brushing his and he felt a crackle of energy, flashing back to the hospital and how she'd lightly touched his bicep, the only place not bandaged. Even broken and sore, he'd relished her warmth and softness. The touch had meant to comfort, but instead it stirred something in him that he couldn't define and didn't know how to answer.

He wasn't a man that settled down, and yet she made him yearn for a life he hadn't lived or known.

It was a shame he wasn't younger and less scarred.

It was a shame he'd lost his trust and innocence as a sixteen-year-old.

Eyes narrowed, he slid the key into the lock and turned. The door opened easily.

Sadie groaned behind him. "You made that look so easy."

He felt his lips quirk and he glanced back at her, taking in the high cheekbones, the angle of her jaw, the fullness of her mouth. She was so beautiful. One in a million, this angel girl.

"After you," he said, pushing the door open.

She stepped into the house, turning on lights as she crossed the threshold. "It's not very big," she said, "but it's got everything. You'll be comfortable."

It was on the tip of his tongue to tell her that he knew,

that the house was his and he'd placed it with Marietta Properties to manage for him, but somehow he knew it'd just end up flustering her. Far better to let her do her job and then sometime, another time, he could tell her when she wasn't all pins and needles.

"Not sure if you remember, but this is one of the original buildings from frontier Marietta," she said, closing the door behind him and heading across the open floor plan to the kitchen. "A couple years ago someone bought it and converted it into a rental house. It's really popular and almost always booked."

Rory followed her to the island, glad to see that the small snug house, reminiscent of the early homesteader cabins still dotting Montana, looked just as good as the last time he'd been here, which was well over a year ago. This stable conversion was probably his favorite renovation he'd ever done. He'd insisted that the architectural integrity of the exterior be protected, but the interior had been reimagined with new walls, windows, and roof, stabilizing the historic structure to ensure it'd survive the harsh Montana winters for another hundred years. Inside the old stable, reclaimed lumber and salvaged materials gave the new living room, bedroom, kitchen, and bath comfort and style.

"There's coffee in the canister next to the espresso machine, and milk in the fridge," she added, placing the key ring on the creamy marble-topped island. "If you have any problems, don't hesitate to call the office. I'm sure you have the number, but here's one of the company business cards just in case." She pulled the business card from her coat pocket and set it next to the key. "Any questions?"

He picked up the card, scrutinizing the name and number, Natalie Hicks, President of Marietta Properties. "How do I reach you?" he asked, looking up at Sadie.

She smiled crookedly and tugged her knit cap lower. "Natalie owns the business. You'll want to deal with her if there's a problem."

"But what if I want to talk to you?"

"Not sure that's a good idea."

"I've made a fortune off bad ideas."

Her lips twisted, her expression rueful. "True."

"In fact, I make bad ideas seem pretty cool."

"I wouldn't go that far."

"No?"

"No." She studied him for a long moment, her faint smile fading, leaving her beautiful features stark and somber. "You have a death wish, Rory Douglas, and it scares me so much."

"Every bull rider does."

"Maybe, but most guys wise up sooner. No one stays in the game as long as you."

"I like life on the road."

"Because you don't know how to settle down."

He didn't protest. There was no point. She was right.

"I was hoping you'd tell me I was wrong," she said after a silence that stretched on far too long. "I was hoping you'd learned to deal with your demons."

"Where would be the fun in that?"

"At least you're honest."

"I'll always be honest with you."

She looked away, brow furrowing. "When do you leave?"

"Tomorrow."

"You can drop the key off at the office, or just leave it here and the cleaning lady will return it to us."

"Will do."

She started for the door. His voice stopped her at the threshold. "Just one more question," he said.

She turned and faced him.

"We never talked, but I always felt like you were there for me at each of those events," he said. "Was it true, or was I just being wishful?"

"I was there, but I won't go again. Watching that bull gore you back in August was more than I could handle."

"It wasn't a good night."

"Understatement of the year." She tried to smile but failed, and shook her head instead. "You're a dangerous man playing a dangerous game, and one day it's going to catch up with you. I'm just glad I'm not going to be there when it happens." Then she closed the distance between them and stood on tiptoe to kiss his cheek. "But it was so good to see you once more." She squeezed his arm and stepped away. "Unexpected but rather perfect because it's almost Christmas."

And then with a last faint, wistful smile, she walked out of the snug little house and into the cold white night.

CHAPTER TWO

S ADIE COULDN'T SLEEP. The house was so quiet, far too quiet without Mom—

But that wasn't what was keeping her up.

Yes, she missed her mom, but she couldn't sleep because she couldn't stop thinking about Rory.

Why was he back?

It'd been years since he last returned. Three years to be precise. And he'd only come home then because McKenna was getting married to Phil, but then McKenna's high school sweetheart, Trey Sheenan, interrupted the wedding and kidnapped McKenna and TJ. After the wedding that wasn't, Rory and Quinn Douglas headed to Grey's Saloon on Main Street for a couple of drinks, and most of the wedding party followed. Sadie wasn't a bridesmaid, but she'd helped with the guest book, and so she wandered over, too.

She wasn't one of the regulars that frequented Grey's, but she went that evening because Rory was there. Rory was a magnet. She'd never been able to resist him. That night at Grey's he'd been quiet, letting Quinn and the Sheenan brothers hold center court, but she'd been aware of Rory the entire time. She'd heard him tell one of the girls that he'd be moving back to Marietta soon, and even though those words weren't spoken to her, they'd filled her with relief. If he was coming back, that meant he was leaving the tour.

Finally. Finally, he'd be safe.

Only he didn't mean it. He continued competing, and he continued living on the road, and he just got more injured and damaged every year.

In hindsight, she should have realized he'd been drinking when he said what he did, and he was trying to say goodbye, and it always sounded better to tell people what they wanted to hear.

It wasn't until she visited him in the hospital in Fresno that she realized *she* was the problem, not him.

He'd never asked her to wait for him.

He'd never asked her to care.

He didn't even know who she was.

That was when she gave him up. Not him, of course, because she'd never had him, but the idea of him, and the hope that he could find life, and meaning, beyond the circuit.

And now, just when she thought she'd moved on, he was back, and she was tossing and turning, sleepless and conflicted, two things she shouldn't be since she'd vowed to stop thinking and caring about him. Unfortunately, old habits were hard to break, and she'd been obsessing about Rory since she was thirteen.

Annoyed, Sadie tossed back the covers and left her bed, yanking on a thick sweatshirt over her pajama top and then pulling sweatpants over the bottoms before heading into the dining room. She'd turned the small dining room into her workshop since the garage was freezing this time of year.

Picking up a sheet of sandpaper, she sat down in front of the small dresser she was refinishing and began buffing off the varnish. Sadie had grown up haunting garage sales, thrift stores, and flea markets with her mother, but the scavenging hadn't been for fun, it was a necessity. Her mom worked as a cleaning woman for the mayor of Marietta and other wealthy people in the nice part of town, but being a cleaner didn't pay much and money was always tight. Her mom never complained, though. She just made do and improvised. When rich families discarded throw pillows because the seam was ripped, or tossed a perfectly good lamp because the wiring was loose, her mom would repair the pillow and rewire the lamp and then she'd sell them, making a small profit. Those small profits added up and paid for repairs on their station wagon and new shingles to patch their old roof.

When Sadie was too young to be left home, Mom would sometimes take her to work and give Sadie tasks, showing her how to remove burn marks from a dining room table, or how to remove scuffs from glossy, white baseboards and trim with a little bit of white cleaning powder and a soft damp cloth.

It was inevitable that Sadie would learn how to renew

and refurbish furniture and fabrics. She'd grown up salvaging goods, and it turned out she had a good eye for design and so when she wasn't flying for Big Sky Air, she made headboards and coffee tables and painted dressers that were snapped up the moment she listed them on her Montana Rose website. It was a fun and flexible second job that helped supplement her income.

But refinishing furniture now just made her miss Mom more. It wasn't the same without her. The house needed noise and activity, as well as the smell of something delicious coming from the kitchen. Pumpkin pie. Roast chicken. Pork chops and spiced apples. The house needed a family. Correction, *she* needed a family. She wanted children.

Love.

Sadie put down the sandpaper and exhaled slowly.

She was thirty-five, and she'd been so sure she would have at least a couple of children by now. Instead, she was wide awake, sanding an old dresser in the middle of the night, to stave off loneliness and heartache.

It was her own fault she was still single.

Plenty of men had asked her out, and she'd tried dating, she had, but her heart wasn't in it because none of them were Rory. None of them were as handsome, as rugged, as dedicated. Or as destructive.

Taking a soft cloth to the dresser top, she wiped away the fine layer of dust before gently running her fingertips across the dresser surface. It was finally satin smooth. Ready for fresh paint and her magic.

Friends had asked her over the years if it was difficult refinishing furniture and she'd always said no. It seemed she had a gift for turning something scarred and damaged into something beautiful.

Maybe that was why she'd hung on to the dream of Rory for so long.

THANKS TO HIS pain meds, Rory fell asleep as soon as his head hit the pillow but he was awake early, and once awake he wasn't going to fall back asleep. It didn't help that his very first thought was Sadie, and just thinking of her made his body hum and ache.

All these years he'd looked for her, and it had never once crossed his mind that she was from home.

It was almost laughable to realize that the woman who'd haunted him for years was from Marietta, the one place he didn't want to go or be.

He'd replayed that last conversation with her at the hospital over and over, and it never changed.

He could still feel the pain as he gradually came to, his wrapped wrist and fingers slamming into metal bars and then the hard plastic frame of the hospital bed.

That was when he realized he hadn't died and was trapped somewhere in a dark hospital room. He muttered curse words, as rough and dirty as they came.

"I've just rung for the nurse," a low voice had said from the right side of the bed. "She should be here soon."

He was pissed off and agitated. "Is it dark in here, or is something covering my eyes?"

"Both."

"Why?"

"The doctor is supposed to cover that with you—"

"If you're not a doctor or a nurse, then who are you?"

She didn't answer right away which just made his head throb more. "You're not from the tour, are you?" he snapped, "because I don't need a babysitter."

He understood why the front office needed to manage some of the riders, but he wasn't one of the athletes in need of handling. Despite his injuries, he showed up, and he did the job he'd been hired to do, which was to put on a good show and keep the fans happy. Rory was popular with the fans too, as he could always be counted on to show up for the signings and events, spending time with everyone, from taking pictures with the old ladies and young girls to kissing babies and posing with young cowboys.

"Not with the American Extreme Tour, no." She hesitated. "I'm Sadie. Sadie Mann." She hesitated again as if giving him time to put the pieces together.

"Do I know you?"

"I'm a friend of Mc—" She broke off, failing to finish.

"Mick who? I don't know a Mick, do I?"

"Maybe I got it wrong." Her voice was faint as if she'd

moved away from his bed. She hesitated a moment. "You're lucky to be alive."

"Don't need a lecture now." His voice was sharp, but he didn't care. He knew bull riding was dangerous. It's why he did it. He also seemed to be good at it. At least, good enough to still be alive and bringing in money. Sometimes not very much money but sometimes quite a bit, and money was money, even if he earned it between emergency room visits. "So how did you say I know you?"

"I didn't."

He heard the bruised note in her voice. He'd hurt her. Rory tensed, which just made him hurt all over.

He didn't need this now. He didn't need the guilt or grief—and then he stopped himself as he pictured dark red hair, high cheekbones, and wide serious eyes. It couldn't be the woman from the arena, could it?

"Let me get the nurse." Her fingertips brushed his bicep, warm skin against skin, sparking something hot and elemental within him. Then she was gone.

He waited for her, that night, and the next day, and the day after that, but she never returned.

He didn't know why she didn't come back, and he'd tried to find her, looking her name up on the internet, and there were thirty-one Sadie Manns, and eighteen Sadie Mans, and fourteen Saydee Manns, and it just went on from there.

He even tried to call a couple of them but it was an exercise in futility and humility, and after the third awkward call he gave up, not because he'd given up on finding her, but he figured she'd find him when she was ready.

But it wasn't easy waiting for her to appear. He wanted her more then he'd ever wanted any woman, which didn't make sense because he knew nothing about her. But maybe desire didn't have to make sense. Maybe desire was just that… His need didn't make sense, but then, maybe desire never did.

Just seeing her last night stirred the attraction, waking the desire. It'd be easy if he could write the attraction off as pure lust, but it wasn't just his groin that ached, his entire chest felt tender, his rib cage so tight that every breath bruised.

He didn't even know Sadie Mann, and yet she was his. He'd known she was his every time she'd showed up at one of the stadiums and arenas. And if that wasn't crazy, he didn't know what was.

He hadn't come back to Marietta for her. Heck, he hadn't even known she was from here, but maybe it was fate that brought him back. Maybe he was supposed to know her and make things right with her. Because God knew he didn't need this apartment complex the bank of auctioning in the morning.

His usual investments were still structurally sound and in a good part of town. This complex was on the wrong side of the tracks, anchoring Farrell and Chance Avenues, two streets that no one chose to live on if they could live somewhere else.

Rory made an espresso in the kitchen and then opened his laptop to review the details of the apartment complex. It had been vacant for over two years now. From the photos, it looked fairly decrepit. Local kids had done a good job vandalizing it.

He didn't want it.

He didn't.

He didn't even know why he'd driven all this way from his ranch in Wyoming to look at it. It was a waste of time and energy—

But maybe he did know.

Rory closed the computer.

Maybe the apartment complex was the tool... the opportunity.

If he hadn't come for the auction this weekend... if he hadn't booked the rental house... he wouldn't have found Sadie.

If he hadn't come, he'd be looking up the definition of desire again and wondering why he couldn't forget her. Desire. *Want. Wish. Crave.*

No longer interested in crunching numbers again, or playing out the different scenarios for purchasing and renovating the building, he showered and dressed and headed to his truck, his cane essential in the icy morning.

After clearing the snow off the windshield, he drove the

four short blocks to Main Street, parking on the virtually deserted street. It was only seven, and all the stores were closed, with only the bakeries, diner, and Java Café open on a Saturday morning.

With two hours to kill before the auction, Rory parked in front of Java Café. The café was as quiet as the street and the tall, lean teenager working the counter gave him a nod but didn't try to engage in small talk after taking Rory's order.

Rory was glad for the lack of chitchat. Driving down Main Street stirred a lifetime of memories, more parts bitter than sweet. It wasn't Marietta's fault that he didn't like coming home. The town and people had been nothing but good to him, embracing him and his sister and brother, but the sheer amount of love the folks showed the surviving Douglas kids, undid him.

Rory was at his best when he didn't feel. He preferred to be analytical, not emotional. And Marietta always made him emotional. It was why there were three things he avoided—

Christmas.

Marietta.

And Marietta during Christmas.

He wouldn't be here this weekend, either, if it hadn't been for the auction.

A young couple with a baby entered the café, and Rory turned away from the counter to face the Christmas tree in the corner. Paper ornaments covered the tree. On the back of each paper ornament was a carefully handwritten tag. Rory flipped the tags on the ornaments closest to him:

Boy 8 years old, love sports, a football would be a perfect gift.

Girl 12, loves to read, a gift card to the local bookstore would be ideal.

Boy 6, loves Lego and Star Wars and is hoping for a Lego Star Wars this Christmas

Girl 16, just had her ears pierced and would love a jewelry box of her own

Rory faced the counter again, stomach knotting. All those kids, with all those needs. They weren't even dreams, but ordinary wants and hopes, and it made him uncomfortable.

Everything about this town made him uncomfortable.

He hadn't always dreaded Christmas. Growing up, he'd loved the holidays, and enjoyed the Christmas traditions from ice skating at Miracle Lake, to caroling with his church youth group, to the annual Marietta Stroll. The Stroll was one thing his family did together, and it was a big deal to come to town and splurge on a rare dinner out.

Although his dad was a rancher, they weren't one of the big, successful ranches in Paradise Valley. Their acreage was small compared to their neighbors, and what they did have was rocky and arid because his folks couldn't afford to improve it with better irrigation.

As the oldest of five kids, Rory knew his parents depended on him, not just as another pair of hands on the ranch, but to set the example for the younger ones. Part of being a good example meant not asking for things his parents couldn't afford, and not to be envious of the Carrigan girls with their horses, or of the Sheenan boys with their cars and trucks. Part of being a good example meant focusing on the things that mattered—love, faith, family.

Rory tried to remember this when he saw Trey and Troy Sheenan tearing down the road in yet another new car. But every now and then the envy and frustration got the better of him, just as it had the summer before his junior year of high school when his parents explained they couldn't afford to send him to college. They needed him home to work the ranch, and they hoped he'd understand.

He told them he did. And they'd hugged him, telling him what a good son he was, but underneath he was angry. So very, very angry.

Why couldn't his parents manage their money? Once upon a time, the Douglas Ranch was profitable. Once upon a time, the Douglas Ranch was one of the biggest properties in Montana, taking up a sizable chunk of the valley. But that was before the Great Depression cut the Douglas Ranch into hamburger patty size.

Rory hated the financial struggle. It was why he'd decided early on to be smart about his money, and, from the beginning, he'd invested his winnings, putting aside ninety percent and living off the ten. It meant living frugally, but he didn't mind. As an adult, he had few needs, and he liked being able to provide for his Aunt Karen in Livingston, as well as set up college savings accounts for TJ and McKenna's new baby, a little girl. No future Douglas should be denied the chance to get a higher education.

"Egg bacon bagel sandwich," the tall, young man at the counter called.

Rory went to the counter to collect his egg sandwich and coffee. He shifted his cane as he took the plate and cup, and after thanking the teenager headed for a table. But instead of sitting down, he reached into his wallet and drew out a dozen crisp bills and returned to the counter.

"Did I mess up your order?" the teenager asked.

"No. I'd just like to make a donation to cover those ornaments on that giving tree. Are you collecting the money here?"

"Which ornaments?"

"All of them."

The teenager stared at Rory, dumbfounded. "You want to cover all the wishes?"

"Hopefully this will cover them," Rory answered, handing over the ten one hundred dollar bills. "But if it doesn't, I want you to let me know, okay?"

"How do I find you?"

"You know McKenna Sheenan?" Rory asked.

The gangly teen nodded.

"I'm her brother, Rory. Just tell McKenna what I owe, and I'll take care of it." And then Rory went to his table and sat down with his sandwich and coffee. He could feel the teenager looking at him, but Rory kept his head down and focused on eating.

He hadn't done anything all that remarkable. He just hated thinking of local kids struggling, suffering, especially at the holidays.

Rory chewed with effort. It wasn't easy swallowing with a lump in his throat. It didn't help he kept remembering his family, and Christmas on their ranch.

His mom and dad scrimped and scraped every year to provide the gifts for the stockings and under the tree. There weren't lots of gifts for each of them, either. Instead, they each received one special gift, what his mother would call the 'big gift' and sometimes it was a big gift. Sometimes it was truly a surprise, and Rory remembered each of those 'big gifts' he'd gotten. One year it was the brand new catcher's mitt, the mitt he was certain he'd never get since it was practically the one professional catchers used. Three years later it was his first new bike, a black ten speed that was slick but also completely impractical for ranch life. And there was the last Christmas gift, the car stereo his folks got for the old work truck, which had become his truck, a gift he'd appreciated every single day as he drove his brother and sister to school in Marietta, and then on the occasional date night.

He was driving that truck, stereo turned up loud when he'd returned to the ranch after dropping McKenna off at a sleepover in town. He'd been singing along to a Garth Brooks song when he pulled into the drive and spotted Quinn bleeding out in the driveway. That discovery had been just the first of many.

After all the funerals he'd traded in his truck, and he'd never listened to Garth Brooks since.

Rory pushed away what was left of his bagel sandwich. He wouldn't be able to eat another bite now. The memories were always the strongest when he first returned. He had to be patient. He had to just get through the next twenty-four hours.

The door opened on a gust of wind. Two old men entered, talking loudly about the Stroll taking place that night. They hadn't even finished closing the door when it opened again, with another bracing blast of frigid air.

Sadie entered the café, long copper hair swirling, blowing across her face. Laughing, she plucked curls from her eyes and peeled back another tendril from her lips.

Rory watched her laugh her way towards the counter, eyes bright, cheeks glowing pink. She greeted the boy at the counter with the easy familiarity that came from living in a small town. If you didn't already know everyone, you soon would.

For the first time in forever, Rory felt envious of those who lived here and were happy here. Sadie seemed happy here. He was glad. Marietta was a good place to call home.

Sadie said goodbye to the boy at the counter and turned from the counter, with a big pink cardboard box, on her way out. She was halfway to the door when she spotted Rory.

Emotions flickered across her lovely, expressive face, one after the other. Surprise. Pleasure. And then anger.

"We seem destined to keep bumping into each other," he said easily.

She wasn't half as comfortable. "It's a small town," she answered somewhat stiffly, pushing back yet another flyaway tendril from her cheek. It was stubborn and clung to the corner of her lips, and she peeled it away with a soft sigh of annoyance.

He, on the other hand, admired the curl. Lucky little devil to curl across her lips.

"You're up early," he said.

"I'm heading in to work. Had to pick up muffins for the office. I open on Saturdays."

"Where's the office?"

"Thankfully, just across the street as I'm running late." She shifted the box from one hand to the other. "Everything okay at the rental house?"

"Great."

"That little heater works well, doesn't it?"

He leaned back in his chair, studying her. She hadn't smiled since she spotted him at his table. "Why do I make you nervous?"

"You don't." Her mouth opened, closed. "Okay, maybe a little."

"Why?"

"It's complicated."

"I've got time."

"I'm already late, and Natalie is a stickler for punctuality."

"Then how about lunch?"

"I don't take lunch on Saturdays, but even if I did, what is the point?" Her gaze hardened, her expression suddenly fierce. "You're not going to stick around, are you?"

"Would it make a difference if I did?"

For a split second, she looked young and full of hope. And yearning.

The words *want, wish, crave,* whispered through his head.

"Was there a point in you coming to see me ride?" he asked quietly.

"It doesn't matter anymore."

"It does to me."

"I have to go." And then with a small nod in his direction, she was off, out the door and then quickly crossing the street.

Rory sat forward as the door closed behind Sadie.

If she was anyone else, he'd be done. He didn't chase women. He didn't need women. He didn't need anything from anyone.

Or so he'd thought for all these years.

Rising, he stacked his dishes, coffee mug on top of the plate, but before he could carry everything to the dish bin against the wall, the teenager was at his side.

"I've got it," the young man said, taking the dishes from Rory. "And thanks, Mr. Douglas. For today's donation and everything else you've done."

Rory felt a peculiar pang in his chest. "I haven't done much."

"That's not true. I know you're the one that does the scholarship every year so that local kids can attend different sports camps, and you sponsor other scholarships, too—"

"It's not a big deal."

"It was for me. Back in middle school, you paid for me and two of my friends to go to a special basketball camp in Bozeman. It was amazing. We couldn't have afforded it without the scholarship."

The pang was back. "Do you still play basketball?"

"Yes, sir. I play for Montana State."

"You're a Bobcat?"

He nodded. "I'm just a freshman so not seeing a lot of playing time yet, but coach said I will."

"Good for you."

"But that's thanks to you—"

"No, son. That was all you. Your hard work and your discipline."

The kid held out his hand. "Just so you know I'm grateful."

Rory took the boy's hand in a firm shake. "I know." And then releasing his hand, Rory headed outside.

Exiting the café, he stood on the sidewalk breathing and out, letting the clean frosty air calm him.

Marietta wasn't all bad.

Nor was it all pain.

Marietta could be a good place if he let it.

Maybe he could replace the bad memories with new ones.

Maybe.

"Uncle Rory?"

It took him a second to register that a hand was tugging on his coat sleeve. Blinking, he glanced down at the small boy next to him with the mop of dark brown hair and bright blue eyes. A scrap of shocking yellow peeked from the coat collar.

Rory grinned at his nephew and gave him a quick hug. "You here alone? Where's your mom and dad?"

"Home. But I'm not alone. I'm with my scoutmaster. We're cleaning Main Street to get it ready for tonight's Stroll." He lifted the gray plastic garbage bag and gave it a shake. Cups and cans rattled inside.

"You guys in trouble?"

"No. It's a scout service project." TJ hesitated, his lightly freckled face scrunching. "So are you still mad at Mom?"

"I'm not mad at your mom."

"She thinks you are."

"Your mom knows I love her."

"Then why haven't you come to see the baby?" TJ's smile was gone, his expression painfully earnest. "She told Dad you came to see me the minute I was born and Carolyn Grace is ten months old."

Rory didn't answer right away, silently repeating McKenna's baby girl's name over in his head. *Carolyn Grace.* Carolyn was his mom's name, and Grace was his baby sister's name.

He'd found his mom in the living room. Grace had been killed in her crib.

His throat squeezed closed. Rory couldn't speak or swallow. So much for his optimism about thinking good memories could chase away the bad ones.

TJ's hand covered Rory's where it clutched the cane.

"She's a really good baby," TJ said quietly, urgently. "She's smart, too. She already knows a bunch of stuff and is walking all over the place. Dad had to put locks on everything because she loves to pull all the pans out of the kitchen cupboard."

"You sound like a really good big brother," Rory said, finding his voice.

"Trying to be like you. Mom said you were the best—"

"That's not true."

"Well, she said it. And I believe it." His chin notched up and his blue eyes locked with Rory's. "And you're here, aren't you? You've come to see everybody for Christmas."

Rory's chest was on fire, and yet he pulled the boy in for one more hug. "I'll come over tonight—"

"Not tonight, Uncle Rory. It's the last night of the Stroll, and we're all going. Want to come with us?"

Rory grimaced. "Not sure how much this hip would like strolling in the cold."

"That's true. Maybe tomorrow. That way you could sit in Dad's Lazy-Boy chair and put your feet up."

"I don't think I want to take your dad's chair."

"It's okay. He doesn't need it as much as you do." TJ glanced behind him, noting the kids with their trash bags gathering on the corner. "I better go. See you tomorrow?"

"I'll see you tomorrow."

"Is that a promise? Can I tell Mom?"

"Yes, you can tell her, but TJ, I was never mad at her. I just was working—"

"Then bring a really nice present for Mom so she knows you weren't ignoring her, okay? 'Cause Mom thinks you're still upset about what she said about you riding bulls."

And then TJ gave him a last hug before darting across the still deserted street, his oversized trash bag flapping at his side.

CHAPTER THREE

S HE DIDN'T KNOW why she was at the window, spying on them. It was the thing kids did, and gossips. And yet she couldn't tear herself away from the glass where she was watching Rory talk to his nephew.

TJ looked so happy to see Rory.

Everyone would be so happy to see Rory.

She wasn't the only one in this town who loved him. Rory Douglas meant a lot to a great many people.

A lump filled her throat as she watched the boy give Rory a last hug before running back to join his troop.

If only her feelings for Rory could be so simple. She missed the days where it was just a thrill to see him. She missed uncomplicated hero worship.

Sadie didn't even know when a girlish crush became un-requited love.

Her mom used to tease her about loving someone who didn't even know she existed, but Sadie would just laugh it off, replying, *"We'll see."*

But her mom was gone, and it had been Sadie who was wrong. Her mom died without ever seeing Sadie marry, or

start a family. Her mom had badly wanted to be a grandmother. But not half as much as Sadie wanted to be a
mother.

Sadie released the curtain and returned to her desk, determined to put Rory from her mind.

She was supposed to be over Rory. She had to be over
him. She'd already seen the fertility specialist, and they'd
come up with a plan to help her conceive in the New Year,
and the plan didn't include Rory.

Stick with the plan, she told herself, turning on her desk-
top computer. It's better this way. You're so much better
without him. Calmer. Stronger. More settled.

Better to be realistic.

Better to be mature.

RORY LEFT DOWNTOWN, traveling to Front Street, and then
over the railroad tracks, intending to swing by the apartment
complex he'd be bidding on later this morning, the one
between Chance and Farrell Avenue, close to the Catholic
church and the primary school.

The most direct way to the apartments would be down
Chance, but Rory made a point of avoiding the street
because there was a house on Chance he'd made a point of
avoiding. That house was the last place he'd been before his
life had changed forever.

It crossed his mind as he idled at the corner that he

hadn't helped the pain by burying it so deeply. He'd suppressed all memory and emotion as if nothing bad had happened. But how was it possible to erase a tragedy like the one that had taken place at his home?

So even though he'd smashed the past, it found a way to creep back in through dreams, and dreams that turned to nightmares.

He could go months, even years, without one of the dreams, but eventually, he'd wake up, clammy and sick.

Why hadn't he been there when it happened? He might have given his family a chance or at least saved one of the younger ones.

One day he'd be man enough to take a drive down Chance and face the boy he'd been.

And maybe, God help him, he'd one day forgive himself for not dying.

Chest aching, eyes burning, Rory eased his foot off the brake and passed Chance, taking a right on Farrell instead, driving down the narrow residential street until he reached the empty apartment complex built in the 1960s.

The complex was beyond ugly. Not ugly like the ugly concrete high-rises in urban areas, but the ugly of indifference. This two-story sixteen unit complex had been built for poor people, folks who apparently didn't merit a green space or a playground.

His narrowed gaze swept the graffiti and boarded up windows. The parking lot was nothing but buckled metal.

He wished he hadn't come. He didn't like anything about this complex, but the building inspector had said the foundation was solid and the majority of the walls intact. Electrical and plumbing would need some updating, but the majority of his costs would be in new windows, new doors, new finishes.

On the plus side, multifamily apartments were a solid investment. Fewer apartment buildings were being constructed now than in the past due to the soaring building costs, and with a staggering number of baby boomers heading into retirement, seniors wanted flexibility and options, which made apartment living attractive. At the other end of the spectrum, young adults weren't confident enough about the economy to want to purchase their own homes, making them ideal candidates for apartment living.

Climbing out of the truck, he walked around the property, careful not to step on any of the broken bottles littering the snow-covered lawn.

If this complex was on the other side of the train tracks, over by the high school, it would have been snatched up by an investor. The apartments between Main Street and Bramble were in a desirable neighborhood, but this neighborhood was important, too. This neighborhood had a school and church and good people in it. Renovated, this apartment building would lease.

Renovated, this complex could be fantastic. Sixteen families would have a decent place to call home.

Wouldn't that be worth it?

Wouldn't it feel good to give something back?

That was the question that always motivated him to action. Wouldn't it feel good to do something good?

Wouldn't it feel good to be someone good?

Could this eyesore be the answer he was looking for?

SADIE KNEW A split second before the door opened that he was there. She'd never called it a sixth-sense, but she did have a special awareness when it came to him.

And then the front door to Marietta Properties swung open and Rory's big frame filled the doorway, his shadow blocking the sunlight.

Her pulse skipped as he walked towards her, wearing his trademark black felt hat, his honey brown sheepskin coat open over a dark blue denim shirt.

He was so very appealing in every way. Even though she didn't want to feel this spark, it burned inside of her... awareness, hope, desire.

She'd liked him for so very long. He'd been part of her heart forever. She'd begun praying for him the night his family died, and she'd prayed for him every night since. Twenty-two years of prayers. Twenty-two years of believing that love and faith could help, and heal, and that love and faith would bring him home, and maybe give him peace.

"Turning in the key to the rental house?" she asked, trying to sound calm, not easy when her stomach was lurching, and her pulse was leaping.

She didn't love him anymore.

She didn't.

But she could still want the best for him.

She could still want him happy.

"No, I've decided to extend my stay. Your website said it's available through the holidays, so I'm going to book it through Christmas Day."

"You're sure?"

"I called Natalie already, and she said I just needed to swing by and take care of the paperwork."

"I see."

"You don't know anything about the paperwork, do you?"

Rory had been appealing this morning at the café with the shadow of a beard, but now with a clean jaw, he looked devastatingly attractive, even more handsome now than he had as a teenage boy, and he'd been the hottest guy at their high school, with his thick, shaggy dirty blonde hair, piercing blue eyes and that gorgeous face of his, chiseled jaw, lovely mouth, and just a hint of a cleft in his square chin. Girls had adored him, not just because he was a great athlete, but because he was kind. Polite. Chivalry personified.

And that was even before the terrible thing that happened on their ranch.

Everyone in Marietta called Rory a hero for saving his

brother Quinn, but Rory never viewed himself that way. McKenna told Sadie that Rory blamed himself for not saving the others. *Survivor's guilt*, Sadie's mom had murmured when Sadie shared the information with her.

"It's usually standard paperwork," Sadie answered, trying to focus. "But since you already filled out the rental application, I'm not sure what else she'd want you to sign. I can give her a call."

"I think she's on her way in. I'll just wait."

"Here?" she squeaked.

"Is that a problem?"

"No. No. I just didn't want you to be… bored."

"I won't be. It's nice just to be in out of the cold."

"Would you like a cup of coffee or tea?" She gestured to the narrow sideboard behind her with the coffeemaker and the platter of muffins. She'd bought a dozen this morning, and a dozen remained. "Or a muffin?" she added. "As you can see, we still have plenty of those."

"I do like a good muffin," he said, perfectly serious, and yet his blue eyes glinted at her. "But maybe just coffee."

"It'd certainly warm you up faster," she said, jumping up, and then almost bumping into him when he made a move towards the coffee pot. She took a quick step away. "I've got it," she said. "You relax. Maybe in one of those chairs." She pointed to the row of chairs outside Natalie's office. "They're far more comfortable then they look."

"I'll just wait here," he said. "If you don't mind."

"Of course I don't mind. You're the customer." She positioned a Marietta Forever mug on the burner, and then placed a dark roast coffee pod in the machine and turned it on. "How do you like your coffee? Black, or with milk and sugar?"

"Black. And I don't mean to put you to work."

"It's fine. I'm just stapling and answering the phone when it rings." Sadie winced at the breathless note in her voice.

She had to pull herself together. He was here to take care of business, not see her, and yet just being near him made her feel giddy and dizzy. This was exactly why she'd never found the nerve to actually approach him. Close, he was gorgeous, but from afar, he was the most intimidating thing she'd ever seen. Tough, hard, fearless, dangerous.

"Has it been busy today?" he asked.

She was glad for the question. The drip-drip-drip of the coffee had suddenly sounded too loud. "No, it's been pretty quiet. Everyone's getting ready for the Stroll tonight."

"Are you going?"

"No, I can't. I have too much to do. The practical thing is for me to stay home and get caught up so I can get everything in the mail next week."

"But why be practical?"

She checked the coffee cup while fighting a smile. "Playing devil's advocate, are you?"

"I just have a feeling that practicality isn't your strong

point."

"How do you figure that?"

"You're the woman that would appear at venues all over the country. Not sure how you accomplished that, but I wouldn't say it was the most logical thing to do."

Heat rushed through her, warming her cheeks. "You're right. I have a reputation for being impractical and idealistic, but this fall I turned over a new leaf. I'm imminently more sensible now."

"That's quite a change."

The brew button turned off.

She lifted the cup off the burner and carried it to him, careful not to brush his fingers with hers. "I know. It hasn't been easy. I liked being impractical and romantic, but it's time to grow up. If I don't do it now, I never will."

"I think you are perfect as you are."

Sadie returned to her desk and sat back down. "You don't know me."

"I'd like to get to know you."

She adjusted her keyboard and then the desk phone. "I want you to know that I'm flattered. I am. But it's… too late. I'm committed to being responsible and doing what needs to be done."

"That doesn't sound very fun."

"I don't think life's meant to always be fun."

He studied her for a long moment. "What's our story?"

She looked up at him, puzzled. "What do you mean?"

"There's something here between us."

"No, there's not. We're both from Marietta. I'm merely a fan."

"It's more than that."

"I like bull riders. Is that what you want to hear?"

"Bullshit. You liked me."

A lump filled her throat. "Maybe I did. But that was before. Your accident in Clovis cured me."

"And yet I'm here, fine."

"You're here, but I wouldn't say you're fine. You're hurt. And from the way you limp, I'm fairly certain you're still in pain."

"You know, I kept waiting for you to come back."

"Rory, I can't do this."

"Why?"

"I'm here at work. I have to finish these packets. Natalie needs them for the Stroll. She's passing out candied nuts and packets of new listings."

"If that doesn't scream festive, I don't know what does."

Her head jerked up and she met his gaze. He stood with his feet planted, his jaw jutted and his bright blue eyes skewering her. The man looked beyond gorgeous as well as primed for a fight.

"Is that sarcasm?" she asked carefully.

"I've been told I have a dry sense of humor."

"Hmph."

"Find another stapler and we'll finish your packets together."

"Natalie would have a fit if she found you stapling listings."

"You're not allowed to get help when you're behind?"

"Not help from you. You're her man crush."

"Her *what*?"

"She has a crush on you."

"I'm sure that's not true."

"Would you like to see the calendar hanging in her office? It's a photo of you from the Extreme Tour four years ago. I do believe you are Mr. July."

"There is no 'Mr. July'. My photo was the month of July."

"It's been four years, and yet you're still there, above her desk, front and center."

"You're not as sweet as you look," he growled.

"Looks can be terribly deceiving."

"Indeed." His teeth flashed white, his smile rakish and lethal. "You better find a stapler as I'm sticking around until we've got this confusing relationship of ours sorted."

"There is no relationship."

"There is, or you wouldn't be so damn prickly."

"Please leave. You're going to get me fired."

"Not if I call Natalie and explain—"

"You wouldn't do that!"

He shrugged and reached for his phone, retrieving from the front pocket of his jeans. "Calling my bluff?"

"No," she said, watching him scroll through his contacts. "By the way, does she know you and Ron Douglas are one and the same?"

"I don't think it's come up."

"Perhaps you'll want to tell her—"

"Don't worry about Natalie. I'm more concerned with you. We need to talk. We should have talked years ago."

"But we didn't. And now it's too late. I meant what I said last night. I've given you up. Sworn you off."

A tiny muscle twitched near his mouth. "Come again?"

"You heard me. Don't make me repeat something so humiliating." And it was humiliating. She'd spent nearly all of her life thinking about him and dreaming about him, and she couldn't be that pathetic woman anymore. "But if you're desperately in need of company, you're in luck. I see Natalie's car pulling in. I'm sure she'd love to have lunch with you."

"You're the only one I want."

"There's no need to torture me."

"I think it's the other way around, sweetheart. For two and a half years you traveled all over the country to watch me compete, without ever once introducing yourself—"

"You barely knew I was there."

"I *always* knew you were there. I can tell you every city you came to see me in, and I can probably remember everything you wore."

A shiver of sensation darted through her middle. "You

didn't ever try to speak to me."

"How could I? You never stayed for the whole event. You'd come, and then disappear."

True, she thought. But that was because she always got scared.

"So why didn't you talk to me?" he added. "Why run away without ever introducing yourself, or giving me a chance to know you?"

"Because I had this crazy idea, and it was so crazy I never knew how to tell you."

"Why don't you just tell me now?"

"Because it doesn't matter anymore."

"If that's not a game—" He broke off as the front door opened and Natalie entered the small office at full speed.

Spotting Rory, Natalie's eyes widened, and she skidded to a stop. "Oh! Oh. H-h-hello," she stuttered. "It's Rory Douglas, isn't it?"

"Yes, it is, ma'am," he answered, taking off his hat and tipping his head.

Natalie glanced from Rory to Sadie and back again. "What can we do for you, Mr. Douglas?"

Sadie took pity on her employer. "Rory Douglas is also Ron Douglas, who rented the little stable house on Farrell. He said he talked to you earlier about extending the dates of his stay?"

"Yes, he did." Natalie's forehead furrowed. "But if you're Rory, not Ron, then that's your own house. And in that case, there's no need for any additional charges."

"I don't want you to lose the income from not being able to rent it over the holidays."

"It's a slow period for us. Summer is the peak season. And I'm not going to charge you our management fee. That's ridiculous. It's your property. I'll just invoice you the cleaning fee when you leave."

"You do a great job managing my properties," he answered. "Thank you."

"I'm just delighted to hear you'll be in Marietta for the holidays," Natalie answered. "It's been awhile, hasn't it?"

His head tipped. "Too long." Rory glanced at Sadie. "Did you say where you wanted to go for lunch?"

Sadie gave him a death glare. "I can't, I'm sorry. I have too much to do. Natalie needs the packets for the Stroll."

"You've done plenty already," Natalie said. "Go. Besides you're almost off anyway. Don't you leave on Saturdays at two? It's nearing two now. Go! Enjoy! It's not every day we have Rory Douglas home for the holidays."

"Good thing, because all of Marietta would have to shut down and celebrate," Sadie muttered.

Rory just smiled at her, a slow, hot, smile that made her pulse thud. "Maybe I need to return more often," he said.

"We can only hope," Natalie said before shooing Sadie towards the door. "Go. Get. Have fun."

Sadie rose from behind the desk. "Let me get my coat."

Rory gave her another one of his excruciatingly sexy

smiles. "I'll be outside waiting, babe."

Babe.

Darlin'.

Sweetheart.

The man was full of sugar sweet endearments, but she didn't trust him a bit, she thought, watching him leave the office to wait on the sidewalk out front.

He might walk with a cane and a limp, but his tight Wrangler jeans hugged his lean hips and butt, wrapping dense, hard muscle in dark denim.

With the clear blue sky and temperature hovering in the low thirties, he ought to be freezing with his big sheepskin jacket open, but he acted as if the weather was balmy and he was immune to the cold. And maybe he was because he'd survived years on the professional bull rider circuit and continued to compete—and win—when guys half his age had already retired.

Now she was supposed to go have lunch with him and act like it was no big deal when she could barely look at him without her heart racing and her mouth going dry and every intelligent thought deserting her. Rory Douglas was over-whelming in every way. Just talking to him last night and this morning had made her nervous and giddy, breathless and dizzy. She shouldn't melt when he talked to her, but she did. She shouldn't lose her backbone when he focused his piercing blue eyes on her, and yet right now she felt warm and tingly and spineless. Not attractive for a woman her age, and she was a woman, not a girl. She was thirty-five. She should be mature and rational—and she was, actually—except when it came to him.

He was her weakness.

Her kryptonite.

Which meant lunch with him was going to be danger-ous.

THE FRONT DOOR to Marietta Property opened and closed, and Sadie marched towards him, snapping her puffy coat closed. Rory heard her short, indignant huff as she dragged her knit cap over her gleaming hair.

"I'm not happy with you," she muttered, yanking on her gloves as she faced him.

"Because I outmaneuvered you?" he asked.

"You didn't."

"Oh, I did. And it's because you have no strategy, where-as I do."

"I am not going to even dignify that with a response."

"That way," he said, touching her shoulder, and pointing towards the end of the street.

She glared at him but fell into step beside him.

"And I think you very much need lunch because you are seriously hangry—"

"I'm not hangry," she said, forced to pause at the corner to wait for a car to pass. "I'm frustrated. You can't just make someone have lunch with you."

He took her elbow as they crossed the street wanting to be sure she wouldn't slip on the patch of ice in the middle of the road that hadn't yet melted. "I personally believe you want lunch with me, but I think you struggle with confidence, and as confidence has never been one of my issues, we're finally having that first date we should have had two and a half years ago."

She tugged free as they stepped up on the curb on the other side of the street. "That's not it at all. I've simply made other plans, and you don't factor into them." She glanced at him then. "I'm sorry if that hurts your feelings."

"Feelings aren't hurt. I always like knowing where I stand with a woman."

"Good."

"But am I allowed to know how I once factored into your plans?"

"You're better off not knowing, and I'm better off not discussing them because it just makes me realize how ridiculous I was. Happily, all that is in the past."

Rory didn't understand why his gut burned, or his chest tightened. How could he be angry? He didn't even know her, and yet there was a small part of him that was offended that she'd moved on. Quickly, too, apparently.

Sadie drew another quick breath and smiled brightly. "Just consider yourself off the hook."

"Maybe I don't want to be off the hook."

"You don't even know what I wanted from you."

"Hoping it had something to do with you."

"It did. In a big way. But it wasn't realistic, and that's why I can't spend time with you. I can't risk getting close to you. I'm still in recovery." Her smile shone even brighter now if such a thing was possible. "I might always be in recovery."

"Recovery from what?"

"You." Her laugh wasn't quite steady. "I'm sure you figured this part out. I fell for you years ago and spent far too many years harboring this secret crush. Carrying a torch for you. It was childish and impossible, and instead of outgrowing the infatuation, the way most young girls eventually do, I just kept... caring... and hoping."

"You make it sound like a crime."

"It kind of is." She reached up and tugged on her cap, drawing it lower. Her voice dropped as well. "I've spent my adult life waiting for you, and it wasn't until my mom died that I realized I was wasting my life, losing out on opportunities I might not ever have again. So I let the dream of you go so I could move forward. And I have. I'm going through my first round of ART right now and with any luck, should be pregnant in the New Year."

"What did you just say?"

"I'm using a donor and doing ART. Artificial reproductive technology—"

"I know what ART is. It's frequently used for breeding

bulls."

"Oh, good. A lot of people don't know—"

"But why?"

"I want to be a mom."

"On your own?"

"My mom raised me on her own and we did fine."

He felt as if he'd just gotten a good kick to the head because nothing she was saying made sense. "Who is going to be the dad?"

"I've found some good donors through the Bozeman fertility clinic."

"Donors."

"I've narrowed it down to three men. I just need to pick which one, but I've time. The procedure isn't scheduled for a couple of weeks."

He stared at her, dumbfounded. "What about men? You've just written them off? No more dating? No more relationships? No more sex?"

"I'm dating," she answered.

"Does he—or they—know you're trying to get pregnant?"

"I'm dating just one man right now and he does know. I've told him."

"And?"

"He understands that if we get serious, he's getting a package deal."

"That's crazy."

"No more crazy then me chasing you all over the country because I wanted *your* baby." She gave him a pointed look. "Because that was my brilliant, nonsensical plan. I wanted *you* to get me pregnant."

For a split second he couldn't think of a single thing to say, and then he exhaled. "Let me try to get this straight. You were coming to see me because you wanted my... sperm?"

Her jaw flexed, expression almost flinty. "Go ahead, laugh. Everyone else has."

"I'm not laughing." Rory was struggling to wrap his head around everything she'd told him. It was strange, and beyond unsettling. It also didn't make sense. If she'd really wanted him to knock her up, she would have just slept with him right away. But she'd never tried to seduce him. She'd always kept her distance. "Why me?"

"I-I just thought you'd be the perfect... donor."

His brow creased. "Darlin', I didn't even know your name."

"I'm sure you bedded some of your buckle bunnies without knowing their names."

"My buckle bunnies," he repeated almost savagely, increasingly pissed off.

Color flooded her cheeks. "But I didn't want a hookup. I didn't want to be a one-night stand. That's why I kept losing my courage, and why I couldn't approach you. You were on this reckless path, determined to make an early exit, while all I wanted was to try to keep a piece of you alive."

He didn't know if he wanted to punch something or grab her and hold her close. He was angry and frustrated and confused, too. She had the strangest way of making him feel things he didn't want to feel. "How would having my kid help anything?"

"Because I'd have a part of you. You wouldn't be totally gone. You'd still exist—"

"This is nonsense, Sadie."

"Maybe to you, because you have no idea how wonderful you are. You place no value on your life, and can't seem to care that people really, truly love you and if something happens to you, hearts will be broken. My heart will be broken. Yes, you're tough, and you've survived a lot, but you're not immortal, and you're not replaceable, and when you're gone my life will never be the same. That's why I wanted your baby." Her tears were falling so fast she couldn't catch them all. "I wanted something of you to love and cherish when you're no longer here—"

He grabbed her and pulled her to him, kissing her to stop the stream of furious words. Her lips were cool, and yet her breath was warm, and he wrapped an arm low around her waist, anchoring her to him so that he could more fully explore her soft, warm mouth. She tasted sweet and fresh with a hint of mint, making him think of a candy cane.

He deepened the kiss, wanting more of her sweetness and warmth and softness. She felt right in his arms, achingly familiar, and it crossed his mind that she felt like home, whatever that meant.

But then she pushed against his chest, not hard, but just enough for him to know he had to let her go. Reluctantly he released her, and even more reluctantly stepped away.

"Not fair," she choked, looking up at him with bright dark eyes, soft pink lips, and flushed cheeks, "You can't kiss me like that when I've given you up!"

"Well, maybe I haven't given you up."

"You never had me—"

"Oh, darlin' I've had you for years."

Her eyes widened with outrage, and she turned away, but he wasn't having it. He pulled her back into his arms and kissed her again, and the moment his lips covered hers, he felt a jolt of pure energy race through him. She must have felt it too, because she shivered and leaned into him, pressing herself close, her arms wrapping around his neck, holding him tightly.

He urged her even closer, using his hand in the small of her back to bring her hip to hip, chest to chest. Sadie felt so right in his arms—fierce and fragile and impossibly alive.

"Somehow we're doing this all backward," he murmured against her mouth.

She murmured a protest, and he took advantage of her parted lips to taste and explore the sweet heat of her mouth. Her full lips quivered, and his tongue stroked her lips and tongue. She shivered against him, and he grew hard, hungry with desire and need.

He wanted her, and he wasn't going to share her at all. He'd fight any man who wanted to try to take her from him.

"Ahem," a sharp, pinched voice sounded behind them. "Do you think that's really appropriate here?"

He knew that voice but couldn't place it. Lifting his head, he eased his hold on Sadie, but he wasn't about to let her go. And then he spotted Mrs. Bingley, practically vibrating with disapproval, and he smiled. "Hello, Mrs. Bingley," he said. "How nice to see you."

Apparently, it wasn't the greeting she'd expected, and for a moment the older woman was too flustered to speak, and then she managed to string a few words together. "Is that you, Rory Douglas?"

"It is, ma'am. Beautiful day, isn't it?"

Mrs. Bingley again could find nothing to say, and instead, she focused her attention on Sadie, giving her a contemptuous glare. "Sadie Mann. I'm shocked. I thought your mother raised you better!"

Rory expected Sadie to wilt. Instead, her jaw firmed, and her dark eyes blazed. "She did," Sadie answered. "But now that she's gone, I'm just doing what I want."

Carol Bingley's jaw dropped. "Well, I never! Your mother must be turning in her grave."

"Not that you'd know where that is. You didn't go to her funeral. And she only worked for you for what, twenty-two years?"

For a moment there was just shocked, uncomfortable

silence, and Rory knew he'd better take action before this turned into something truly ugly.

He squeezed Sadie's waist, pulling her even closer to his hip. "Happy holidays, Mrs. Bingley. Do give my best to Mr. Bingley. And I hope he enjoyed the tickets to the show in Billings." And then he began walking, dragging Sadie with him, wanting to put as much distance as he could between his volatile redhead and Marietta's biggest gossip.

Chapter Four

Sadie's heart was racing and her body was trembling. She didn't know if she was more upset about Mrs. Bingley's rudeness, or Rory's bone-melting kiss.

The problem was, his arm was still around her, and his body was so warm, and yet hard, and yet perfect, and she couldn't seem to get her brain back, or her strength.

The man could kiss, and that kiss…

So good. So hot. And exactly how she'd imagined Rory would kiss. It made her furious, though. How unfair of him to kiss her now when she'd decided to only pursue solid, dependable, manageable men. And maybe Rory was solid and dependable, but he certainly wasn't manageable.

"Now that is just playing dirty," she gritted, pulling away from him after they'd walked a good block. But the moment she pulled away she missed his warmth and the hard, muscular contours of his body. He might need a cane, but he was built like a high-performance machine.

"How so?"

She began walking again, needing to move to somehow escape all the emotions swirling inside of her.

Of course, he fell into step next to her. "You're such a coward."

"How so?"

"You won't talk, you can't face me, you just want to run."

"Maybe that's because I'm in survivor mode."

"Well, toughen up, darlin'. Life's hard and you need to be just as strong."

"You don't know me."

"I know you're hurt, angry because you lost your nerve. Instead of coming to the arena and introducing yourself, you'd watch and run away. You're upset because you never gave me a chance to get to know you, and now that I'm here, and want to know you, you've decided it's too late."

She stopped abruptly, hands balling. "It *is* too late!"

"You're upset," he continued calmly, "not with me, but with yourself. You wish you had the *cajones* to go out with me, but you are still afraid to actually live. Far better to fantasize your way through life—"

"I don't have any grand fantasies about you! For your information, you're not on a pedestal, and I don't think of you as a superhero."

"Maybe not a superhero, but I must have been some kind of wonderful for you to want my baby."

Sadie had no answer for this. She glanced away, jaw grinding, temper stirred.

"Maybe it's time to stop running," he said quietly.

"Not running anywhere," she answered tightly, staring at the courthouse with its dome glimmering in the sun. "If anything, I stopped running. I gave up flying. I'm staying put so that I can have the life I wanted—"

"This isn't the life you wanted. Let's *at least* be honest about that. You had feelings for me long before you got it in your head to have my kid. Being a single mom was never your dream."

"Stop acting like you know what I want."

"I do. Because I was there at those arenas, and I saw how you looked at me. Darlin', I wasn't a sperm donor. I was a man, *your* man—"

"You have such an ego."

"So it was all a game? Showing up at stadiums and arenas, making me feel as if you were there for me—"

"It wasn't a game. I *was* there for you! I went to see *you*."

"Then why write me off without even giving me a chance?"

"That's not how it is," she protested, heart hammering, hot tears stinging the back of her eyes. "I'd never write you off. I couldn't."

"But you won't even talk to me, or have lunch with me."

"It's called self-preservation, Rory." She looked at him now, pain splintering her heart. "I made you such a big part of my life, and it was too big. You took over my life, and it wasn't healthy."

"Is that why we can't even be friends? According to this

new leaf you've turned, you can't even talk to me."

"I'm talking to you now."

"It's like pulling teeth."

She moistened her lips with the tip of her tongue. "I don't know *how* to be friends with you."

For a long moment, there was just silence. Rory's gaze narrowed and he glanced at the ornate façade of the old Bank of Marietta, one of the first brick buildings constructed on Main Street in the 1880s. "Have you even tried?" he asked, his deep voice pitched low. "Or am I really going to be dead to you?"

Pain rolled through her, making her ache all over because he knew far too well what dead was, and loss felt like, and it hurt her to think that she might be hurting him. "Please don't say it like that."

"Maybe you discovered I'm not who you thought I was. If that's the case, just tell me. I'm man enough to handle the truth."

Sadie felt as if she'd swallowed something sharp. Her insides hurt. Her stomach cramped. How could she lie to him? It was impossible.

"There's nothing about you I don't like, Rory," she said hoarsely. "But I just don't know how to be friends with you. We've only seen each other from afar. We've projected all sorts of things and who knows what's real or true?"

"But isn't that what we should find out?"

"I'm not sure how."

"Talking is a good start."

"I didn't think men liked talking all that much."

The corner of his mouth lifted faintly. "We can talk when we have to."

"Is this a have-to-situation?"

"It's more of a want-to-situation. I want to know you, Sadie."

She drew a careful breath, trying to slow her wildly beating heart. It had been a hard four months. She'd lost her mom. She'd lost him. Or at least the dream of him. But now he was here, and he wasn't a dream. He was tough and demanding and completely overwhelming. "Where do we start?"

"We've already started. We just keep going."

"You're kind of intimidating in real life, Rory Douglas."

"Take it in baby steps," he said.

"And what is a baby step?"

"Lunch. I'm starving."

Some of the tension in her chest eased. "Actually, I'm hungry, too. All those tears and confessions."

His lips quirked. "Emotions can be draining."

"Spoken like an expert."

"Now you're just being sassy."

"Maybe a little bit." She smiled and glanced around. They were almost at the end of Main Street. "What about Main Street Diner? They specialize in comfort food."

"I don't know if I need comfort, but I am craving some

of their homemade cornbread."

"If I ate that I'd have no room for pie."

"Are you planning on having pie?"

"Of course. Why else go to the diner?"

"Well, there's the meatloaf, and pot roast, and chicken pot pie and—"

"And apple pie, cherry pie, peach pie, chocolate cream, banana custard, lemon meringue…" Her shoulders lifted and fell. "I've never been able to deny myself a slice of good pie."

"Why should you? Life's too short not to enjoy the good stuff."

THE DINER WAS half empty, and a waitress seated them in the big corner booth with a view out both windows. "I always wanted to sit at this table," Sadie said with a sigh, leaning back and relishing the space. "We could have a party here."

"Who would you invite?"

"Well, McKenna, of course, because she's a lot of fun, and Taylor, the librarian whose married to Trey's twin, Troy. And you, obviously, because you were the Extreme Bull Rider Tour's Mr. July four years ago."

"I was never Mr. July."

"But you were a centerfold."

"I was a photo on a calendar. That is all."

"Mmm."

"What about Natalie? Are you two close?"

"No, but I like her. She's a good boss. She works really hard. It was her dad's business, you know. She used to work for him, and then when he wanted to retire, she took it over. She's trying to make a go of it, but her dad made a lot of poor decisions, and so it hasn't been easy trying to turn it around."

"What do you do there?"

"Just administrative stuff. I'm only supposed to be part-time, but when she's slammed, it can turn into full-time."

"I hope you get paid for those extra hours."

"I get health insurance, and that's huge. I'll need it when I'm pregnant, for maternity care and everything."

His smile faded, and he regarded her with a rather brooding intensity. "How will you manage when you have the baby?"

"I have my business. I can do it from home." She reached for her phone and scrolled through her photos. "This is what I love to do." She turned the phone around to show him, quickly clicking through a series of photos of tables, chairs, dressers, headboards. "I buy salvage pieces and then make them into something new." She then scrolled further. "And this is my new thing. I've started to make pillows out of vintage fabric, and it's been really successful. The Christmas ones sold out within a week."

He took the phone and looked through the pictures more slowly, studying each of her designs. "Where do you sell them?"

"Through my website, The Montana Rose, and I also have a couple local stores that have started carrying pieces. They want my pillows but those are easy to pack and ship myself, so right now they're only available through my site."

"You don't want your own retail space?"

"Maybe one day, but I can't afford the overhead, and frankly, I don't want to be tied down with regular hours and staffing. I like the freedom of working out of my garage, and with the baby—" She broke off, smiled tightly. "It's good to be independent, you know?"

"I do, and you're talented."

"Thank you." Sadie took her phone back and turned it off, slipping it back in her purse. "I like being creative, and I love being my own boss."

"How did you get it into it?"

"I've refinished furniture for years. I started back in high school." She looked at him a moment, just taking him in, still amazed that they were sitting here together, talking about life and jobs as if they were a couple on a first date. But this wasn't a date, and she had to be careful not to let her imagination run away with her. Much less her ridiculous idealistic heart. "What about you?" she asked. "What do you do when you're not on tour?"

"Stop by my ranch, make sure it's still there, and then check on my real estate, take care of any repairs are necessary."

"Doesn't sound like you spend much time at your ranch."

"Not if I can help it."

"What's wrong with it?"

"There is nothing wrong with it. But there's nothing"—he shrugged—"right with it, either."

"Why did you buy it?"

"I thought it'd be a good investment, but as it turns out, it was just okay. I've been more successful with rental properties. They're solid. Tangible. I like putting my money into something I can touch."

"Do you have a license?"

"No. And unless I'm buying at auction, I use a broker. I don't like all the paperwork. Happy to give a commission to someone willing to handle that for me."

"Is it rude to ask what have you've bought?"

"A couple apartment complexes in Bozeman, another two in Missoula, I have one in Billings, and then some rental houses as well." He leaned back as the busboy brought them two glasses of water. "It's actually what brought me to Marietta this weekend. An older apartment complex over by the Catholic church was being auctioned this morning—"

"The one on Fourth Street between Chance and Farrell?"

"You know it then?"

"Natalie's dad used to own it. He struggled to keep it leased, and so he sold it to someone else and then it ended up in foreclosure. It's been abandoned for some years now."

"Three," he answered, "and I think it has potential so I came for the auction—"

"I hope you didn't buy it—"

"I did."

"*No.*"

"I was the only one who showed up to bid."

"Because everyone else knows better," she muttered.

"Or maybe everyone else was too afraid to invest in the community."

"It's not easy trying to sell that part of Marietta. It's considered undesirable."

"It doesn't have to be."

"You say that because you weren't raised over there. I was, and I know it's a hard sell. One of the reasons I moved into my mom's house after she died was because I couldn't get a fair price for it. Natalie tried to sell it for me, and she got lowball offers, and so rather than take a pathetic offer, I let my apartment in Bozeman go and moved back home. As it turns out, it's been a good decision because her house was paid off, and I don't have a mortgage and am saving quite a bit of money, but you... I don't envy you trying to turn that complex into something appealing. There's a lot of crime over there."

"Like what? Kids on skateboards carrying spray paint cans?"

"Grafitti is a problem."

"Thank you for the heads-up."

She knew he was laughing at her and she sniffed. "I hope you got a good deal."

"I did. It was a *great* deal."

The waitress arrived to take their order. Sadie waited for her to leave to ask, "How did you get started in real estate?"

"A former girlfriend convinced me it was better to invest in real estate instead of letting my money just sit in the bank."

"Sounds like she was a serious girlfriend."

"We were together a number of years."

"What happened to her?"

"What always happens, the relationship ran its course, and we parted ways."

"Just like that?"

"Darlin', every woman I dated knew upfront I didn't do forever."

"So you never loved any of them?"

"I cared for them, and I loved making love to them—"

"*Not* the same thing!"

He smiled at her, a smile so slow and hot and sexy that it seemed to suck every bit of oxygen from the room. "You've never made love to me."

Sadie struggled to catch her breath. He was big and imposing from afar, but close like this, he was positively lethal. "Nor will I. I'm not looking for sex."

He grinned at her, white teeth flashing, creases fanning from the corner of his eyes. "Are you quite possibly a thirty-year-old virgin?"

Sadie considering tossing her ice water at him to knock that smug smile off his gorgeous face. "*No.*"

"It's okay if you—"

"I'm not. I've had serious boyfriends, and a fairly long-term relationship that my mom hoped would turn into the 'one', but it didn't."

"Why not?"

"Turns out he was seeing a couple different flight attendants at the same time."

"That must have been devastating."

"If I'd loved him. But I didn't." She grimaced. "My mom took it hard, though. She thought he was Mr. Wonderful."

"Was he that wonderful?"

"He'd bring her flowers when we had dinner with her. She loved that."

"What kind of flowers would he give you?"

"He didn't."

"Why not?"

"I don't know." She grimaced. "Maybe he was too busy giving them to his other girlfriends."

"At least you can joke about his other girls." Rory leaned back against the booth. "Have you ever been in love?"

She took a quick drink of her water. "Just once."

"What happened?"

Her shoulders shifted. "Nothing. I never told him."

"Sounds like you need to take more risks."

"While you, Rory Douglas, need to take less."

CHAPTER FIVE

R ORY HAD AVOIDED relationships ever since he and Krissy broke up a couple years ago, but even with her, he'd made it clear he wouldn't ever get married, or start a family. Commitment wasn't for him, or so he thought until he sat listening to Sadie talk about getting pregnant and having a baby on her own.

He didn't like it. He didn't like anything about it. And he would have never called himself old-fashioned or judgmental, but thinking of Sadie trying to raise a child on her own got his back up. He wanted more for her. He wanted more for the baby, too. Life was challenging, and children deserved as much security and stability as possible, which was why having two, loving parents was far more ideal than just one.

"So what is your pregnancy plan?" he asked. "Have you started any medicine? Is it going to be an IVF procedure?"

"The doctor doesn't think we need to try IVF right off the bat. He has me on Clomid, and I'm tracking my temperature, and I also have an ovulation kit, too. When it's time, I'll go in and he'll transfer the donor sperm and, fingers crossed it'll work." She gave him a bright smile. "It might take a couple tries. I'm prepared to give it six months, and if that doesn't work, then we go to IVF. That's why I'm trying to save everything I can. Just in case IVF is necessary."

"What about the men you're dating? Anyone special?"

"It's good… but you know, still in the early stages."

"What's the problem?" he asked.

"There's no problem. Paul's a decent guy. He really is."

"You don't sound very excited about him."

"We're still getting to know each other."

"That doesn't sound encouraging, sweetheart."

"He's a solid, stable man. He's a Marietta city planner. His office is at the courthouse."

"I don't care about his resume. I want to know how he makes you feel. Does he light you up? Is it hard to keep your hands off him?"

Her lips compressed primly. "I'm not fifteen, Rory."

No, she wasn't fifteen. She was a gorgeous, smart, passionate woman in her thirties and she deserved a man who'd make her feel beautiful and valuable and cherished. "So there are no sparks and no chemistry?"

"There could be. If I give him a chance."

"Chemistry doesn't work like that."

"I've heard it can develop over time."

"How many dates have you had so far?"

"Four."

He made a low, rough sound. "I don't get it. You want

to park me in the friend zone—and we have chemistry off the charts—while you keep dating him, hoping something will develop? Why?"

"Because he's here, and you're not."

"I'm here now."

"Yes, but for how long? You avoid Marietta like the plague."

He ground his teeth together, unable to argue that.

Sadie continued on, expression defiant. "After Mom died, I made a vow that I'd give other men a chance, and that's what I'm doing."

Rory refused to even let himself imagine her on a date with Paul, or anyone else. She was his, plain and simple, and while this wasn't the time to follow that thought all the way through to its conclusion, he knew he'd have to examine it later. But for now, he was fighting for her, and fighting to claim her. "Has family always been important to you, or is this something that's become more urgent since your mom died?"

"I always planned on getting married and having kids, lots of kids. It's actually something of a shock to realize here I am, thirty-five and still single. I don't mind the single part as much as I mind not being a mom. That's so important to me."

Rory could picture her pregnant, glowing. She'd be so bright and beautiful. He swallowed hard to chase the vision away. "Your mom didn't put pressure on you to settle down?"

"Never. She only ever wanted me happy. And, yes, she wanted grandkids, and I wanted to make her a grandmother. I thought there would be time." Her voice quavered, and she drew a quick tremulous breath. "She was a wonderful mom. She would have been a doting grandmother."

"Any brothers or sisters?"

"No, just the two of us. My father died when I was a baby—he was a trucker—killed during a winter storm in Wyoming during one of those infamous whiteouts. I don't remember him, so I've never really missed him, but I know Mom did."

"She never remarried?"

"She never even dated again. Said she loved Dad too much." Sadie paused, remembering. "Growing up, we had our moments, but by the time I graduated from high school, she really was my best friend."

"No wonder you're missing her so much."

"Yeah." She rubbed her fingers in the moisture beading her water glass. "There were certain things we always did together. Holidays like Easter, Thanksgiving, and Christmas, as well as things like tonight's Marietta Stroll. We went every year together. It was our annual tradition."

"Is that why you're not going tonight?"

"No. I need to work. I really am behind."

"Are you behind, or are you just pushing yourself too hard?"

"I need to make money while I can."

"You need to honor her memory."

Suddenly her eyes shimmered with tears. She dashed them away before they could fall. "I'm afraid if I go, it will just make me sad."

That soft, tearful confession felt like a vise around his heart. He didn't know how she did it, but it felt as if she'd climbed into his chest and taken up residence there. "What if I took you?"

Her head dipped, hiding her face. "You don't want to do that."

"You should know by now that I'm not easily manipulated, or guilted into doing things just because someone thinks I should. I do what I want, because it's what I want, and I want to take you tonight. I think it's important you celebrate your mom's memory." His voice dropped, deepening. "When I lost my mom, I didn't do enough to celebrate her. It was a mistake. Don't be like me."

Sadie didn't immediately speak, and Rory immediately kicked himself for saying what he had. It was a struggle for him to share and be open. His previous relationships had ended because he couldn't, wouldn't open up, and they were right, he hadn't been willing to share many thoughts, never mind feelings. But the past had held him back far too long. If he wanted more out of life, if he wanted the chance he'd prayed for that night in Clovis, California, then he had to try to give more and trust more, even if it felt foreign as hell.

"Well, that would be wonderful," she answered, giving him a watery smile. "I was just worried the cold would hurt your hip."

"I appreciate your concern, but I'm tougher then I look," he answered dryly.

Her head jerked up, brown eyes wide with surprise and then she realized he was teasing, and she laughed even as she cried.

She was a walking disaster, he thought, torn between tenderness and exasperation, but at least she was his disaster.

Rory leaned across the corner of the table and kissed her. Her lips quivered beneath his, soft and salty from tears, and yet her warm mouth tasted impossibly sweet. He didn't think he'd ever get tired of kissing her, which was a good thing since he didn't intend to let her go.

SADIE DIDN'T WANT the kiss to ever end. She felt so good and warm, deliciously warm, and when he lifted his head, ending the kiss, her cheeks burned, and her lips tingled, and she felt exquisitely sensitive all over.

"You have to stop doing that," she whispered, realizing she had no idea how to manage him, and her feelings were most definitely not under control. "People will get ideas." *I will get ideas.*

"Let them. You're beautiful, and I'm enjoying being with you."

Heat flooded her, but also anxiety. The compliment was lovely. *He* was lovely. But wasn't that the problem? Rory made her want the sun and the moon and all the stars, but how was that realistic? If once she started hoping and dreaming again, how would she ever settle for a quiet, normal life without him?

"You don't do forever, remember?" she said huskily, stressed, parched. Her hand shook as she reached for her water glass. She took a long, rather desperate drink to cool off, as well as pull herself together. By the time she set the glass back down she felt calmer and more in control. "Rory, you've no interest in settling down. You don't like feelings. I love feelings. You don't want to settle down and I'm planning on becoming a mom. Our goals and plans don't align—" She broke off when the waitress arrived with their lunch.

Sadie was grateful for the interruption. She exhaled and leaned back against the seat while Rory gave her a look that made her think they weren't done with this conversation.

That expression of his made her nervous. But then, he was making her nervous. Rory brought out the most emotional, impractical, irrational side of her, and Sadie was exhausted from being emotional, impractical and irrational. It was time she grew into the person she was meant to be, the woman her mother raised her to be, which was strong, self-sufficient, and independent. Not teary and fragile and emotionally dependent.

She'd vowed to make permanent life changes, changes that meant she'd use her brain, not her heart, and she'd made good progress by coming back, moving into her childhood home, and working at a local business instead of jetting all over the country. But Rory threatened everything, the stability and peace of mind, she'd worked so hard to achieve.

Rory finished his sandwich before she'd gotten through half of hers. The moment he was done, he pushed his plate back and focused on her. "Are you and this Paul guy in an exclusive relationship?"

Sadie nearly choked on her bite of turkey sandwich, the bread and meat suddenly way too dry to swallow easily. "No," she said when she could speak.

"Is he seeing anyone else?"

"I don't know. I don't mind if he is, though."

"So you're not into this guy at all."

"You can't say that."

"I can. And if you're going to date him, there's no reason you can't also date me."

She put down her sandwich, no longer hungry. "We talked about this."

"I heard what you said. You're determined to go out with decent, boring men to feel like you're keeping a promise you made to your mom—"

"This has nothing to do with my mom. This is about me, and managing my feelings, and I won't be able to do that if I get close to you. Kissing you makes me breathless—"

"Good."

"Not good. Because it makes me want more than kissing. It makes me want everything."

"Even better."

"No! It's not. Don't you see? If I keep kissing you, how will I ever go to Grey's tomorrow night with Paul and watch football and eat wings and pretend I'm having a great time? How will I laugh at his jokes and be appropriately sympathetic when he tells me stories about working for the city and how his boss smells of onions, but it could also be body odor, he doesn't know, and he's not sure if he should say something to his boss, or buy him a stick of deodorant—" She broke off, temper blazing. "Because that's what dates with Paul are like. He's a caring man who takes his job seriously, and is worried about his supervisor's hygiene, and doesn't want to offend him but help him make better decisions."

Rory's gaze met hers and he seemed to be trying hard not to laugh. "So this is my rival?"

"He's not your rival."

"It might be smart to give him a heads-up that he's about to lose you."

"Are you even listening to me?"

"I am. Well, I'm trying to, but I keep getting distracted by your beautiful brown eyes and your lovely lips. I love your lips. They are made for kissing."

"You're not taking this seriously."

"I'm taking this very seriously, so seriously I'm suggesting you never let Paul kiss those lips again."

"You don't own me."

"I don't want to own you. That's not my style. But I'm also protective of what is mine—" He broke off as a pair of boys shyly approached their table, a pad of paper and pen in the older boy's hand.

Sadie swallowed her temper as the younger boy prodded the older boy into speaking, but even then, the older boy, somewhere around nine or ten, was so bashful, he stammered as he asked for an autograph.

Rory immediately focused on putting the boys at ease, making small talk with them for a few minutes, before signing two slips of paper. The boys repeatedly thanked him and then waved before returning to their table, where they showed their father the autograph. The father beamed with pleasure and gratitude, and he gave Rory a small nod, clearly grateful Rory had taken time to be kind. Rory nodded back, and Sadie's chest squeezed impossibly tight.

This man, this beautiful, wounded man that she'd loved since she was thirteen, was turning her inside out. Being near him was like riding a roller coaster—highs, lows, and endless thrills. One moment she wanted to slug him. The next she wanted to hug him. Did he have any idea how frustrating he was?

Did he know how good he was? How generous he was with others? Did he realize that just by sitting here with him, she was falling for him, again?

It was so dangerous. So impossible. She didn't want to hurt him and yet she had to protect herself.

"You were good with those boys," she said tautly, furious with him, and equally furious with herself because her heart felt tender and raw and her body hummed with tension from fighting a dozen different wants and needs.

She could pretend she didn't care, but she would always have feelings for him. Strong feelings. Dangerous feelings.

"I like kids," he answered gruffly.

"And yet you don't want any of your own?"

"I don't think I'd be a good dad."

"Why?"

"I'm not…" He shrugged. "Not selfless enough."

Those words and his indifferent shrug spoke volumes. He wasn't indifferent in the least. If anything he was painfully aware of his fears and needs.

"At least you're self-aware."

The corner of his mouth lifted. "I was sure you'd argue with me, try to tell me what a great dad I'd be."

And he would be, she thought. It's why she'd wanted more than anything to be with him and raise a family with him. He was the ultimate hero, the ultimate protector. He was her ideal man. Sadie's eyes burned, and her throat threatened to seal closed.

She was thankful her voice sounded steady and even. "I think it's better, to be honest than have a family and walk out on them."

His smile disappeared. His chiseled jaw jutted. "I'd never walk out on my family."

"Are you worried you wouldn't be affectionate?"

There was nothing friendly or approachable about him now. His eyes narrowed, his expression flinty. "That wouldn't be an issue, not with me. I'd talk to them all the time, and hold them every chance I could."

"Then what is the problem?"

"I think I'd just love them too much."

CHAPTER SIX

*H*E'D LOVE THEM *too much.*
Those five words said it all, revealing the painful truth of who he was and what he'd lived through and how he'd survived.

She'd known the tragedy had scarred him, marked him, and he rode bulls to escape. He courted danger nightly because it was the only way he knew how to manage the loss and his grief. In that moment, she thought she'd never loved him more, but it wasn't something she could say, or would ever say. He wasn't a man that wanted tenderness, and she couldn't imagine trying to get close to him only to be abandoned later when the intimacy suffocated him.

And so Sadie stayed silent, and when the waitress asked them if they wanted dessert, they said no at the same time. Rory handed the waitress several folded bills to cover lunch, and then they were on the street, saying what felt like a very awkward goodbye.

Sadie was certain he was regretting everything about lunch, from sharing his feelings to offering to take her to the Stroll tonight. She hated to think he now felt obligated. He was definitely not obligated.

"If you want to pass on tonight, I totally get it," she said, stumbling over the words. "It would probably be better if I stayed in and got caught up—" She broke off as he reached for her, tugging her away from the curb as a motorcycle zoomed by.

"You're not backing out, darlin'," he said, releasing her elbow. "I'm picking you up. Just give me the address, and I'll be there."

"Things seem a little weird between us."

"Things are a lot of weird, but we'll sort it out. I'm not worried."

"Today's craziness doesn't throw you?"

"You know what I do for a living, right?"

This was why the man had legions of fans who lined up at venues all across America to meet him. He was successful, determined, and confident. *Seriously* confident. And confidence was sexy.

She didn't want to smile but couldn't keep her lips from curving. "Good enough, but I think it'd be better if we met downtown this evening. I'm checking a guest later, and they're going to pick up the keys and information from the office at six. It shouldn't take long. Ten minutes or so."

"Why doesn't Natalie do it?"

"She has a dinner date, and then she's working the booth on Main Street."

"Fine. I'll meet you in front of your office a little after six."

She started to walk away but then turned back around. "And just to be clear, it's not a date."

He shrugged, broad shoulders relaxed. "You can tell yourself that if it makes you feel better, but you did fine at lunch."

Sadie marched back towards him. "Lunch wasn't a date, either."

"We have kissed several times now."

"You can't take a non-date and make it a date."

"We already did." He reached out and brushed his hand over one of her coppery strands. "And there's no reason to get nervous. Just talk to me tonight as you do your friends. Pretend I'm McKenna. That should make it easier."

"Great. I'll tell you all about the new fabric I found at the Bozeman flea market, and my last date with Paul, and the donors I'm considering."

"Actually, I don't need any more details about Paul. Ordinarily, I wouldn't be into fabric, but I'd rather hear about every yard you bought, then more about your donors."

"But I haven't told you about the three I've selected."

"*Three?*"

She didn't know why, but she was enjoying his outrage. She'd been playing defense ever since he came to town. It was his turn to do some mad scrambling. "I still need to narrow it down to one, but I've time. See you around six."

RORY DID SOMETHING he hadn't done and maybe fifteen years. He left town and drove to Paradise Valley, taking the back roads from the valley floor to the foothills where the Douglas Ranch had been. The property had been on the market for years, but no one had wanted to buy a huge piece of land with such a gruesome history. And because they could survive without selling it, Rory had pulled it off the market seven years ago and it had just sat there, empty. Land without animals. Land without people.

Reaching the entrance to the ranch, Rory climbed out of the truck and unlocked the front gate before swinging it open and driving over the cattle guard back to where the house had been.

He didn't go all the way back—he still couldn't go there—but he went close enough that he could see the roof of the barn, and the shape of the hills behind. To his right was the cluster of poplar trees, his mother's favorite, and not far from the road was the huge boulder that had been the site of the Douglas kids' first clubhouse. It was where they'd jumped and climbed and played, with the big steep face becoming whatever they needed it to be—a sailing ship, a dungeon tower, a cliff rising from the ocean.

His smiled faintly at the memories, glad for the adventures they'd had. And there had been many adventures. Great adventures. Quinn had been the most athletic. McKenna the most imaginative. Tyler by far the best natured. Gordon was rough and tumble, all boy, even at five.

And Grace... well at two she'd still been too young to join in the games.

Sitting in his truck, he said each of their names, and pictured them all, individually, as well as together. It was something he hadn't done in years. It was something that needed to be done. Remembering them, and who they'd been, and how important they'd been to him.

As he sat there, truck idling, he felt waves of emotion. Anger. Pain. Grief. Rage. And after the rage came deep, unbearable sadness.

Christ, he missed them. And he wasn't using the Lord's name in vain. It wasn't said in disrespect, but a prayer. *Christ*, he missed them. And he missed himself. He missed who he'd been, and he missed who he might have become.

He was never supposed to be this hard, isolated man. He'd never been a loner. He'd never wanted a life alone. He'd loved his family so much. He loved the little ones fiercely. When the babies arrived, he was smitten. Enamored. Quinn hadn't his patience, and so when his mother needed a break, she'd hand Rory a fussy Grace, and he'd walk with Grace, walking until she stopped crying and squirming, walking until she'd relax, and then turn her little face to his neck, her mouth pressed to his skin. And finally content, she'd sleep.

It was in those moments when he held her and was able to soothe her, that he understood himself best. He wasn't here to accomplish great things. He was here to live, and love. It sounded so simplistic but he wasn't a complicated person. He loved being on the ranch. He loved riding and working the land. And he loved his family. Those were his great loves. Then they were taken from him, and their deaths broke him.

It wasn't just that they died, destroyed him, it was how they died... slaughtered in their own home.

A year after the funeral, a year after the endless investigation which never turned up a single suspect or produced a single arrest, the house was razed. The area was plowed and he, Quinn, and McKenna scattered wildflower seeds—Indian paintbrush, forget-me-nots, asters and lupines—and they returned later that spring to see how the hillside was covered in purple, white, lavender, and brilliant orange flowers.

They'd said a prayer then, and the three of them had agreed to only remember the good because that was how their dad and mom would have wanted it, but Rory found remembering only hurt more and the pain made him angry. Better to bury the pain, and so he had.

But maybe he'd buried it too deep for too long. Maybe he should have come up here more often and looked to see if any forget-me-nots remained and the pain wouldn't still be so intense.

Better late than never, he told himself, shifting gears and turning the truck around. At least he'd come today. At least he was trying to deal with the past. The emotions didn't feel pretty, but it was a start.

What was it he'd told Sadie outside the diner? Baby steps? Well, he'd taken a big step coming here today, and it was a positive step. Now he just needed to keep moving forward.

AFTER THEIR LATE lunch at the diner, Sadie went home and got to work. She stenciled an elegant gold flourish on the painted nightstand and then, while that was drying, sat down with her sewing basket and finished stitching the blue and cream tassels to a new dishtowel pillow she'd made. Sewing usually relaxed her because her thoughts could drift, but today they were drifting too much. As she worked the needle in and out of the trim, she kept seeing Rory in her head and hearing his voice.

He was not as hard and invincible as he seemed.

Just acknowledging that made her heart hurt. But it also worried her, because she was supposed to be getting over him, not making more space in her heart for him. As it was, she already compared every man to him.

Poor Paul. He really didn't stand a chance, not with Rory back in town. But Rory wouldn't remain in Marietta. He never did. He'd be on the road again soon, and it'd be years before he came back.

Sighing, Sadie tucked the needle through the fabric and tassels one last time before finishing with a securing stitch then snipping the thread, knotting it, and returning her needle to the strawberry pincushion in her sewing basket, the pincushion and the sewing basket a present to her on the seventh birthday from her mom.

She gave the plump base of a strawberry pincushion a little squeeze, and sent up a quick silent *I love you, Mom*. It was still so hard to grasp that her mom was gone and not coming back. The heart attack had come from nowhere. Her mom had seemed so healthy. It was frightening to think how quickly everything could change. How quickly everything did change.

And just like that, her thoughts drifted back to Rory. He was so beautiful with his piercing blue eyes, and crooked sexy smile, and then there was his swagger. She secretly loved his swagger. But beneath that tough exterior of his, he had struggled and while she wanted to help him, she couldn't. His battles were his own, just as her battles were hers. The best way she could help him was by being true to who she was and what she wanted—and that was love, and family.

Sadie carried the finished pillow to the garage where she tucked it inside a large plastic bag with its mate, ready to go out in Monday's mail. And now that the pillows were done, she could think about what she planned to wear tonight.

In her room, she tried on a dozen different outfits. It was going to be cold tonight, so she needed to dress warm, but she also wanted to feel pretty, not easy when her down jacket turned her into a big marshmallow. In the end, she chose an oversized burgundy sweater and paired it with a dark green plaid scarf. She curled the ends of her hair so it did a pretty flip and then ditched the high heels for cozy, fleece-lined boots.

At five-thirty she left her house all bundled up and walked down Second Street until she reached Main. It was dark when she started out, and she wasn't worried about walking alone, but it felt good to reach the Graff Hotel, handsome with its festive, red-ribboned wreaths in every window and fragrant greenery swagged over the front doors.

The hotel's uniformed valet lifted a hand, and she waved back. There were times she missed Bozeman's thriving nightlife and wonderful restaurants, but there were pleasures to living in a small town. Here, people waved when you walked by, and they slowed their cars and stopped for pedestrians, even if the pedestrian didn't have the right-of-way. People just cared. And she liked that. A lot. It's why she wanted to raise her children in Marietta. This was home. It would always be home, with or without Rory Douglas.

PARKING WAS A challenge in downtown Marietta, but eventually, Rory found a spot on Church Street and walked to Marietta Properties. Sadie was just locking up the office when he arrived, bundled up in her puffy coat with a festive green plaid scarf twisted around her throat, the green setting on the bright coppery strands of hair.

"You look pretty as a picture," he said, leaning down to give her a hug.

"You're cold. I have a feeling you had to park far away," she said.

"I did. But it gave me a chance to stretch my legs and enjoy the fresh Montana air."

She laughed, and he tucked her gloved hand into the crook of his arm as they started walking down Main Street. "What's our plan? Where to first?" he asked.

"I think a cup of hot cocoa would be a great start," she said, "and then, once we have our cocoa, we can just wander around, checking out displays and all the shop windows."

Everybody seemed to have the same idea as there was a line out the door at Copper Mountain Chocolates, but people waited patiently for their turn, and once they had their hot chocolate, Rory understood why. It was rich and fragrant and tasted like melted chocolate. "This is the best hot cocoa I've ever had," he said.

Sadie grinned happily. "It is. I have a girl crush on Sage. I love what she's created here in Marietta, and how much she has accomplished in just five years. It's hard to remember Marietta without her store."

They were walking along Main Street, admiring the lights and decorations, as they talked. Couples and families surged around them, the crowd becoming thicker. Three boys chased each other down the sidewalk, and Rory stepped in front of Sadie to be sure they didn't run into her.

"How is it that you went to school with my sister, but you and I never met?" he asked.

The third boy wasn't looking and slammed into the back of Rory and would have fallen into Sadie if Rory hadn't caught him, and swiftly righted him.

"Impressively fast reflexes," Sadie said.

"Now Hammerfall might dispute that, but it's reassuring to see that I'm still faster than an eight-year-old."

She laughed, and Rory felt ridiculously pleased with himself. He was no better than one of these boys tearing down the street, all reckless energy and bravado. "You were going to tell me how it is we never met," he said.

"Oh, right. Well, we never really moved in the same circles."

"But you went to school with Mac?"

"We didn't meet until junior high as I went to Park Elementary and she attended Marietta Elementary."

"So you and I never met, but you knew about me?"

She nodded. "And I kept tabs on you, from the time you joined the PRCA and then switched to the PBR, and then finally joined the Extreme Tour."

"You really did follow my career."

"I absolutely did, and always from afar, until I had a layover in Spokane a couple years ago, and I knew you were competing in Coeur d'Alene, so I rented a car and went to watch you. It was wild and addictive, and after that, I tried to see you whenever I could."

"You've mentioned flying before, and dating a pilot. I take it you were you a flight attendant?"

"Yes. I was with Big Sky for ten years."

"You've given up flying?"

"After my mom died I realized I needed to stay put in one place. And so that's what I'm doing."

"Do you miss the travel?"

"I do. There was something exhilarating about taking off and landing somewhere new. I loved how every day would be different, and whenever I had a layover somewhere new, I'd get out and visit the city."

"And now your wings are clipped."

"They are, but hopefully not forever. If my business doesn't take off and do what I want it to do, I'd have to find something else I could do that isn't a desk job. I have a hard time being in the office all day, makes me feel cooped up."

"But Natalie is a good boss?"

"Yes, and she's been great about giving me time off for medical appointments and stuff like that." Sadie nudged him. "Want to keep walking? If we want to do the wagon ride, we've got to reach the courthouse by eight."

He nodded, and they continued down the street, popping into different stores and then pausing at the corner to listen to a children's choir sing. The kids were completely off tune, with some singing more robustly than others, while one boy covered his face with his music book, and at the other end of the line, a little girl danced in place, oblivious to all.

Rory watched Sadie watching the children, and she was absolutely mesmerized by them, as if these wiggly, out of tune little human beings were the most fascinating things she'd ever seen.

Watching her, he felt a pang. She really did want to be a mom, and she'd be a great mom, too.

He wrapped his arm around and gave her a slight squeeze. "You okay?" he asked quietly.

She nodded, blinking, trying to keep the shimmering tear from falling.

"You'll have your own one day," he said. "It won't be long."

She nodded again, struggling to smile. "I was just thinking about my mom. It's just starting to sink in that she's not coming back."

"Grief isn't easy," he said gruffly.

"I miss her every single day."

The kids finished their song and their vocal director had them moving up a block. Rory drew Sadie away from the crowd and noise so they could talk. "How did she die? Was it an accident?"

"Heart attack. I didn't even know she had any heart problems. She looked so healthy. She worked even the day she died." She bundled her arms across her chest. "I was flying the day she died. She left me a message saying she was tired and going to lie down, that she'd been short of breath all day and maybe she'd overdone it, but she'd be fine, and I shouldn't worry." Sadie chewed on her lower lip. "By the time I'd checked into the hotel with the flight crew and phoned her, she was gone. She'd died that night at home, alone."

Sadie looked up at him, shadows in her eyes. "The last house she cleaned was the Bingley's. And maybe it's unreasonable of me, but I'm so mad at Carol Bingley for not caring more about my mom. I'm so mad that my mom meant nothing to her. You'd think that after twenty years, Mrs. Bingley might have sent a sympathy card or note, or dropped a casserole off, but no. She never said one word to me about my mom, not until today, when she saw us, together." She drew a raw, rough breath. "But if Mrs. Bingley had died, my mom would have been cooking food for Mr. Bingley, and over there arranging flowers and just helping because that's what good people do."

He hugged her then and held her tight, her cheek pressed to his chest. "Your mom was a good person."

She hugged him back, hugging him hard. "She was. She was a great person."

He could tell she was trying not to cry. He could feel each ragged breath, and her sadness made him want to protect her forever.

Finally, she eased herself back and looked up at him, dark eyes still wet. "All I can think about is how I never thanked her. She sacrificed so much for me and I don't think

I ever told her much I appreciate everything she did for me."

He reached out and lightly ran his fingers over her cheek where a tear still shimmered. "Do you think parents want that?"

"I don't know."

"Is that why you want children? So they'll be grateful for your sacrifices?"

She scrunched her nose. "That sounds awful."

"I doubt, then, that your mom kept score."

"Oh, she'd never do that. Not ever."

"So what would she want from you?"

Sadie stared off towards the towering Christmas tree at Crawford Park. "She wouldn't want anything from me."

"Then what would have been important to her?"

She took another minute to think this over, too. "She would have wanted me to live the best life I could."

"Then that's what you need to do." He kissed her brow, covered by her knit cap, and then kissed the tip of her small, straight nose, and then one last light kiss on her full, warm lips. "You thank her by living the best life you can."

SADIE SHOT SMALL glances up at Rory as they crossed Court Street on their way to the Crawford Park where they'd get in line for the wagon ride with all the others already queuing up by the big Christmas tree that went up every weekend just after Thanksgiving.

He'd made her ache earlier when he'd said he'd love his children too much, and now he gave her hope by telling her that her mom would want her to live the best life possible because that was exactly the kind of thing her mom would have said. Her mom wouldn't want anything from Sadie but for Sadie to be happy, and surrounded by loyal, loving friends and family.

"Thank you," she whispered, giving his arm a little squeeze.

He glanced down at her, brow lifting. "For?"

"Bringing me out tonight, and talking to me about my mom. What you said really resonated with me, about me thanking her by living the best life I can. You have no idea how much that helps. Because it's something within my control, you know? It's a choice I can make every day... to live the best life I can."

"Smart girl."

They joined the line winding past the massive decorated tree. Kids were sucking on sticky candy canes while parents clutched coffee cups, trying to stay warm. It was a beautiful, clear night, the wind having chased all the clouds away, leaving the dark sky glittering with countless stars. The trees in Crawford Park were frosted and iced while the Courthouse dome gleamed a brilliant white.

"I can't believe I'm saying this," he said after a moment, "but it's actually good to be back, and I wouldn't be here tonight if it weren't for you. I was trying to remember when

I last came to the Stroll and it was probably my senior year of high school."

"That long ago?"

"You make it sound as if we're talking about when dinosaurs roamed the earth."

She laughed and lightly smacked his shoulder. "Stop it. You know what I mean. And you're not that much older than I am. Just three years, I think."

"The Stroll has changed, though. Main Street still has all the lights and garlands and booths with sweets, but I could have sworn they used to do the judging of the gingerbread competition in the lobby of the courthouse."

"They did. About ten years ago they moved the competition to Bank of Marietta, and now it's at the Graff."

"When I was a kid, Santa used to sit next to the Christmas tree at Crawford Park in a fancy gold and red velvet chair."

"That changed the year we had the ice storm, and Santa refused to sit outside and freeze to death."

"Don't blame him," Rory said, tugging the zipper higher on his coat. "It's cold tonight, and many locals would consider this balmy."

"Does it bother you that Santa and the gingerbread competition are now at The Graff?"

"Why would it?"

"There's been some chatter that maybe The Graff has become a little too involved, and it taking over too much.

But I don't know if that's true. Wasn't the Graff here since the beginning? Yes, the hotel was boarded up for a long time, but my mom remembered going to the Graff as a girl to see Santa, and that was back in the forties or fifties, and I'm sure Mr. Graff must have hosted big holiday events there in the hotel's heyday."

"I think people are just jealous. The Sheenans have done well for themselves."

She darted a quick glance in his direction. "You weren't always a fan of the Sheenans."

"You know about all that?"

"Everyone did at Marietta High."

He shrugged. "I only ever had a problem with Trey. He put my sister through hell, but they've worked it out and Mac's happy, so I'm not going to hold a grudge." He gave his empty cup a swirl. "And this is totally off topic, but this hot chocolate from Sage's shop is so much better than the instant stuff we used to sell in our Future Farmers of America booth."

Sadie laughed, but that was because she remembered the annual FFA booth set up outside the Mercantile and their lukewarm, barely drinkable hot chocolate priced for $1, outrageous considering they only put in two miniature marshmallows per Styrofoam cup. "I'll have to tell Sage. Having belonged to the FFA, I think she'll appreciate the compliment."

In the distance, sleigh bells could be heard, along with

the the steady clip-clop of hooves. The wagon was on its way. Standing on tiptoe she watched the wagon turn the corner, and proceed down Court Street, bells jingling, the big horses moving at a brisk pace. She felt a thrill as the gorgeous horses approached, and then another as the wooden wagon rolled to a stop. The wagon rides had been part of the Stroll since she was a little girl, and every year she and her mom would board for a ride around town.

The bearded driver climbed down from his seat and positioned the stepstool in front of the wagon and began assisting people up.

Sadie flashed Rory a smile as he handed their tickets to the driver. "This is the perfect way to kick off the holidays," she said, trying not to clap her hands, but ridiculously excited because what could be more festive, or more romantic, than a wagon ride with the most handsome man in Marietta?

"I wasn't feeling the holiday spirit before, but I'm getting there," he answered, taking her elbow to keep her steady as she climbed up the stepstool.

He followed her up, grabbed the carelessly folded blanket from the edge of their hay bale and, taking a seat next to her, he covered her legs and lap, tucking the blanket in around her waist.

"Real men don't get cold?" she teased, noticing he hadn't covered his lap.

"I've got you," he said, closing the gap between them so

they were hip to hip, his hard thigh pressed to hers.

A few minutes later they were off, and Rory put his arm around her, supporting her back over the bumps and jolts in the road. Kids in the front were singing "Jingle Bells", and Sadie glanced around, seeing the smiles, feeling the happiness. *She* was smiling and happy, too, and she knew she'd remember this night always. At least, she wanted to remember this night, and so she made tiny mental notes of everything—the bright stars overhead, the periodic jingle of the sleigh bells, the grassy smell of the hay bales, and Rory, next to her, of course.

She stole another glance in his direction, feeling impossibly lucky to have this one night with him. No matter what else happened, she'd always have this memory, and she'd cherish it even more after he was gone.

"If you keep smiling at me like that," he said quietly in her ear, "I'll end up kissing you in front of all these people."

Her pulse quickened, need and desire making her stomach flip. "You're evoking painful memories of Mrs. Bingley," she whispered with mock severity.

His blue eyes glinted with laughter. "If that's not a mood killer, I don't know what is."

"Then I think we should *definitely* keep discussing her."

"So you do want to be kissed."

"By you? Of course. No one kisses like you, but, Rory, I'm going to be a big pregnant lady soon, and you won't find that quite so appealing."

"I think you'll be a very sexy mom-to-be."

"Have you ever seen a naked pregnant lady?"

"Yes."

"Who?"

"Demi Moore, Jessica Simpson, Britney Speaks, Christina Aguilera, Nia Long."

"Oh. On magazine covers." She made a face. "I'm pretty sure I won't look like that."

"And I'm pretty sure most of them had some airbrushing done." His gaze swept over her in a thorough, leisurely inspection. "I'd very much like to see you naked, pregnant or not."

Heat rushed through her, making her tingle from head to toe. "Where is your mind?"

"Sweetheart, I've wanted you in my bed from the first moment I laid eyes on you." He gave her a crooked, wicked smile. "Now, be honest. Haven't you ever imagined being with me?"

Every single day, she thought breathlessly, eyes locking with his. For an endless moment she couldn't breathe, remembering how much she'd wanted him, and how frequently she'd pictured him peeling off his shirt, and then dropping his Wranglers, revealing hard, honed muscles everywhere. Sadie locked her knees together, fighting the flood of desire. "Of course, I did. But I didn't just want to jump into bed with you. I wanted to know you. I wanted to do… this." She gestured to the night and stars and the world around them. "Go places with you, hang out with you, just be with you."

"Like we did today."

"Yes." She blushed, suddenly shy because today was pretty much the perfect day. Well, except for the emotional outbursts and crying jags and hysterical declarations on Main Street. Those she could have done without. "Today was great, and tonight's been nothing short of amazing."

"And tonight isn't over."

"True."

"So, want to tell me about these three donors of yours?"

Sadie nearly jumped out of her seat. It was the absolute last thing she expected him to say. "*What?*"

"I'm curious about what you're looking for in a donor. But there is no pressure. I can understand if you don't want to talk about it with me."

She'd wanted to talk to him for years. She'd wanted a real conversation where she could get his thoughts and opinions, but this was definitely bittersweet. "It hasn't been as easy as I thought it would be. There are thousands of donors. So many options. But I've narrowed it down to three and feel pretty good about them."

"What was your criteria?"

"I wanted someone smart, and strong. Someone with integrity. Ideally, he'd have a sense of humor, too, because you've got to be able to laugh when things get hard."

Rory's lips curved in a faint smile. "Humor is huge."

"But it's hard to know from the profiles if he has a good sense of humor. After all, the people who claim they are funny, are rarely funny."

"This is true."

"So how do I know if he would be as good and kind as he says he is? How do I know that he's generous and supportive of others?"

"I'd think the profiles would include a resume or some kind of list of accomplishments."

"They do, in a vague sort of way. For example, one is a medical doctor and the profile doesn't say where he went to school, or which field of medicine he specialized in, rather it's 'A New York native, #1234 moved to Montana four years ago to practice medicine in Missoula. 6'2" and one hundred and eighty pounds, #1234 is an avid fisherman, rock climber, snowboarder, and spends most of his free time outdoors'."

"Sounds like a catch. Why don't you just go with him?"

"Because there's no mention of his family and if he even likes people. What if he's an athletic brainiac with no heart?"

"And heart's important?"

"Very much so."

"What do you like about him?"

"He's smart and successful."

"Right."

"And the clinic told me he's fairly attractive."

"You don't get to see a photo?"

She shook her head. "No, but the nurse said he's a 7.5, maybe an 8."

"That's pretty good for a doctor. Those guys aren't always attractive."

Sadie stifled a giggle. "That's terrible."

"Hey, I'm not knocking doctors. I appreciate the really good ones. They've put me back together more times than I can count. So what about the other two?"

"One is a high school math teacher, and the other is a professional musician."

"Doesn't sound like you have a type."

"That's the thing. Is there a type for being the best father? I don't know."

"But the donor isn't going to be the father, is he? You're going to be the parent, so does it matter if he's paternal or not?"

Sadie's smile faded, and she tugged on her gloves, and then pulled her coat sleeves down lower. "So you don't think nature has anything to do with it?" she asked carefully, inexplicably blue. "You believe it's all nurture?"

"Sweetheart, I think you'd be happier picking someone you know personally, rather than a stranger from a donor catalog because you'd know his family and how he and his family relate, but since you didn't ask me that, I won't give you my opinion."

"Funny, I could have sworn you just did."

He smiled at her, but the smile didn't quite reach his

eyes, and it struck her that he wasn't quite as relaxed as he'd been earlier. It also struck her that he most definitely had an opinion on who she should pick as a father for her child... or more accurately, who she shouldn't pick.

The wagon turned the corner, and the driver reached for the sleigh bells at his side and gave them a good shake. The bells sounded merrily, echoing off the old brick buildings.

"And which family friend would I go to for this generous DNA donation?" she asked lightly. "Because I'm sure you're not offering yours."

"Friends do help friends."

"Are you seriously considering being my donor?" she asked, knowing he wasn't serious about it all, and certain he'd immediately back off.

But he surprised her yet again. "Maybe I should be."

"*No.*"

"Why not? At least you know me and my family."

"This isn't like fantasy football. We're not drafting an imaginary team here. This is real. I'm going to have a baby, and I'm going to do this soon. So don't make an offer unless you intend to show up at Dr. Crookshank's office in Bozeman and spend ten minutes in a private room with a paper cup."

"And what if I did say I'd show up?"

Her stomach somersaulted, and she laced her fingers together in her lap, forming a tight ball. "Let's not ruin what's been a lovely evening."

"We're having a discussion, not a fist fight."

She squeezed her hands tighter. "What a relief to meet someone just as impossible, if not more unreasonable, then me! All these years I've felt rather crazy, but you're even crazier than me, Rory Douglas."

"And that's why you won't consider my swimmers?"

"Your swimmers aren't the problem. *You* are."

"Me?"

How was it that they were having this conversation while sitting on an itchy hay bale as a wagon loaded with families lurched its way to the Graff? "Yes, *you*. I'm finally getting to know you, and even though I admire you immensely for so many things, I've realized you'd be the worst possible donor because you couldn't handle knowing that I was raising your baby and you weren't part of his or her life. You'd worry about him or her, and you'd feel responsible, and guilt and anger would eat at you, and before you knew it, you'd resent not just me, but the baby."

They were now traveling down Front Street, and he'd been gazing out over the train tracks towards the hotel and depot, and as she talked, she saw how his jaw tightened periodically, the small hard muscle near his ear bunching. But when she finished and fell silent, he turned his head and looked at her, his handsome features relaxed, his blue gaze warm, his expression fond, making her think of an infinitely patient parent who'd just sat listening to the ranting of an emotional teenager.

"How could I resent you if you were my wife?" he asked calmly.

Her jaw dropped. She blinked. Did he have any idea of what he'd just said?

His broad shoulders shifted in an easy shrug. "Seems like marriage is the solution you're looking for. Not a sperm donor."

Chapter Seven

S HOCKED, AND FURIOUS, Sadie disembarked the wagon with the rest of the crowd, but she didn't follow them into the Graff. Instead, she stepped off to the side, knowing Rory would, too.

She faced him, so upset she could barely think straight. "I don't know what you think you're doing—"

"I'm suggesting we marry. I'm suggesting you have that family you want so badly. I'm suggesting you consider giving your baby a real-life *father* instead of just some DNA."

Her chin jerked up. "This is my life, and my future, not yours."

"Maybe it should be."

She stared at him as if she'd never seen him before. Nothing he was saying made sense. Nothing about him made sense. He was supposed to be this distant, detached, unattainable dream, and yet he'd arrived in town and immediately began intruding into every area of her life.

"Maybe you were never supposed to give me up," he added. "Maybe you were supposed to give me a chance so we could make this work."

"How? We don't even know each other!"

"That's just it. We start this thing over. We start at the beginning, not at the end." He seemed to be ignoring her incredulous expression. "We're going to spend time together while I'm here. It's two weeks to Christmas—"

"I am not going to spend the next two weeks trying to cope with you. You are overwhelming in every respect."

"You're afraid of intimacy."

"No."

"Then you're afraid of men."

"I'm not afraid of men. I might be afraid of you, though." She looked away and drew a deep breath, grateful now for his silence. The last thing she needed was for him to mock her. "You are... a lot. You are... big, and tough, and smart... physical. It's a lot to deal with."

"You've had serious relationships."

"Yes, but none of those men have ever been like you." She glanced back at him, expression rueful. "I'm pretty sure there isn't anyone else like you."

"I don't know what that means."

"It means that you could hurt me, and I don't want to be hurt."

"You could hurt me just as easily."

"How? You're the guy that isn't going to settle down—"

"How do you know that?"

"Well, you've told me that."

"No, I've never told you that."

Her mouth opened, closed. She tried again. "But you said at the diner that you used to tell your girlfriends that you didn't do forever. You said you'd warn them off in the beginning so they knew where they stood and wouldn't get ideas."

"Yes, but did I ever say it to you?"

She simply looked at him.

"No," he answered for her. "I didn't because those women weren't right for me. But you very well could be."

For a long moment she just looked at him and then she sighed heavily. "I don't know what to say."

"That's okay. Maybe we just leave it alone for now and go inside and get warm. I don't like to complain, but these old bones are beginning to ache a bit."

As THEY CLIMBED the front step to the grand old Graff, Rory was glad they weren't doing small talk. He wasn't in the mood for small talk.

He'd just suggested marriage, and babies, to Sadie and the crazy thing was, he meant it.

He'd never pictured himself married. He'd never allowed himself to imagine that kind of life... a wife, a home, children. But ever since returning to Marietta, he felt caught up in something beyond his control, as if something or someone else was directing his life, pushing and prodding and instigating change. The strangest part of all was that he didn't mind. If anything, he felt hope. Peace.

Sadie wasn't as calm, though. Glancing at her as they entered the hotel he could see she was in shock.

Maybe even dismay.

She really was overwhelmed.

He didn't blame her. Just twenty-four hours ago she was unlocking the stable house for him, and handing him the keys. And now he was suggesting marriage. Something would be wrong with her if she didn't resist and panic.

"Where do we start?" she asked, tugging off her gloves.

"It's up to you. You know how this gingerbread thing works better than I do."

"No," she said, tucking her gloves into her coat pockets. "This. Us. How do we know if we could be good together?"

"We date. I take you out as my girl, and I treat you as if you're my girl, and we see what happens."

"You're only here for a couple weeks."

"That's all the time we'd need. Let me rephrase that. It's all the time *I* will need. I usually know within a couple dates, and if it works, it works, and if it doesn't, we weren't meant to be."

"And if it doesn't work?"

"Then you're free to continue dating your nice, local, stable men and pursue your ART as you've already planned."

Color stormed her cheeks. "You don't need to sound so judgmental."

"Listen, darlin', I am old-fashioned. I think you're putting your needs before your child's needs and it strikes me as selfish. But I also know you've lost your mom, and you're grieving, and you don't want to be alone."

"This has nothing to do with grief. This has to do with not wasting any more time on impractical dreams."

"Impractical dreams being what? Me?"

"Yes. I pursued you for years—"

"Sweetheart, you never pursued me. I'm pursuing you."

She turned her face away, expression set, and Rory had to fight a smile because right now she reminded him of one of his favorite champion bulls on tour, Sugar, a big red bull with the softest brown eyes but a temper once provoked. Sugar, like Sadie, was equal parts sugar and spice.

After a long, tense silence, she gritted, "What does dating really accomplish?"

"We'll either discover there is something real between us, something we can build a life on, or we'll realize we have nothing in common, and that this attraction, is superficial, based on chemistry rather than anything lasting."

She seemed to struggle with this, too. "How many dates would it take to figure out we don't have anything in common?"

"How many dates have you had with Paul?"

"Four. Five would be our date at Grey's tomorrow."

"Then I suggest five—not for my sake, but for yours, since you seem to need a lot of time.

"That's a lot of time together. That's too much—"

"And yet you've given Paul the same amount of time, and you still don't know how you feel about him."

"Spending time with Paul is nothing like time with you."

"That has to be a good thing."

She shot him a disapproving glance, reminding him of a prim teacher. "Paul is a very nice man."

"Yes, so you've said."

"You know, chemistry can be a problem. The chemistry between us just complicates everything."

"Because I want to have you naked in my bed?"

"That's part of it."

"Darlin', I know you're a city girl, but getting naked is the best way to make babies."

She blushed as only a redhead can.

Thank goodness he'd been raised with a red-headed sister so he was comfortable with spirited women, and knew how to handle them.

"Shall we have a look at the gingerbread houses and see who won what?" Sadie asked stiffly.

She was trying to sound stern, and right now she did look fierce, but she also looked beautiful, a siren with her long, thick red hair, pale, porcelain skin, and expressive dark eyes, eyes that were snapping fire at the moment. "Of course."

"Then let's do it. Otherwise, we'll end up here all night."

He let her lead the way since she'd done this before. The Graff's impressive lobby was crowded tonight, and yet the grand marble columns and rich wood paneling still managed to evoke turn of the century glamour and charm, with a huge fragrant fir dominating the center of the lobby and greenery and wreaths marked doorways and windows. Against the far wall, by the grand staircase was Santa Claus in an extravagant gilded chair, complemented by helper elves.

Rory watched a mom try to place a crying baby on Santa's lap but the infant arched and shrieked, trying to get away. He smiled, remembering that Grace had been the same. She'd wanted nothing to do with Santa Claus, not at her first Christmas, or her second.

He suddenly realized he'd been standing in one spot too long and turned to look for Sadie. She hadn't gone far. She was waiting for him by the first of the gingerbread house displays.

"You okay?" she asked as he joined her.

"Yes, why?"

"You had an odd look on your face."

"That baby… she just reminded me of my sister Grace. Grace didn't like Santa Claus. Wanted nothing to do with him. Ever."

"Does remembering your little sister still hurt?"

He hesitated, letting the emotion fill in, and it was dark and aching, the kind of tender he felt after a bull kicked him in the ribs, but it wasn't the mindless pain he'd feared, the pain that surfaced with the nightmares. "It does. But then, remembering all of it hurts."

"Is that why you don't come home often?"

"It's why I didn't like coming home, but I'm discovering this trip that not remembering actually hurts worse than remembering." He ran his hand across his jaw, feeling the bristles. "I'm going to stop pretending they didn't exist and just let it be what it is."

"Will it ever be okay, do you think?"

"The fact they died? Maybe. But the way they died? No." He looked at her and felt a welling of emotion that had nothing to do with the past or his family, and everything to do with her. His beautiful, sensitive angel who was not quite as sweet as he'd imagined, but which was also good. Rory needed someone with backbone. Someone with imagination and spirit and heart.

"How are your old bones?" she said, slipping her hand into the crook of his arm. "Would they enjoy a comfortable seat in the bar?"

"Possibly."

"Well, the hot chocolate was good, but I have a feeling we're both ready for something stronger."

RORY ORDERED A scotch, neat, and she ordered the Graff's specialty, a delicious hot mulled wine, and for several long minutes, they just sipped their drinks in companionable silence.

It was nice, Sadie thought, the quiet, and the companionship. It was much better than the tension earlier. She didn't do conflict well. Growing up, there hadn't been anyone to fight with as her mom wasn't someone who enjoyed arguing, either.

"You really think we'll know in four dates whether we are meant to be?" she asked after a bit.

"I don't see why not."

He sounded so relaxed and sure of himself, and she wondered how he did it. They were discussing something huge, and life-changing, and yet he didn't seem worried at all.

Her brow creased. "Does today count as one of those four dates?"

"I don't see why not. We did spend a lot of time together today."

"Almost half a day."

"So, yes, it counts."

Sadie chewed on her lip, trying to puzzle this out. "And after four dates, if we're not convinced we work, we do what? Say goodbye? Stop seeing each other…"

"I think we agree we had some fun, and promise to remain friends and move on."

She felt a pang at the idea of saying goodbye and moving on. But was she really ready to think of him as her forever? She'd always dreamed of him as her forever guy, but fantasizing about something and actually having it were two different things. "And you won't be negative about me going through ART to have a baby?"

"I won't be negative in any way. In fact, no one will be more supportive than me."

"Promise?"

"Promise."

"Three more dates," she said, thoughtfully.

"Well, four if you go to Grey's tomorrow because I think it's only fair that you give me the same amount of time as you've given Paul."

"That's ridiculous."

"How?"

"It just sounds… competitive."

"I am competitive. I hate to lose. You've seen me on tour. Surely, that doesn't come as a surprise to you."

"I thought you just had a death wish."

"I still ride well, and win." His features eased, his eyes smiling at her, lips curving. "I'm pretty good at what I do."

"You're twice the age of the new guys."

"That's because they're kids."

"Well, maybe Gramps should think about retiring and doing something a little less dangerous."

He laughed out loud, a warm, sexy rumble of sound. "You've heard the nickname."

"Don't sound so proud."

He laughed again, and this time his rumble of a laugh sent a little thrill through her. "Fortunately, I'm good at a lot of things and have options for the future."

"You're really thinking about retiring?"

"I'm ready to get off the road."

"Where would you live?"

He lifted a brow. "Are we really going to do that?"

"What?"

"Four dates, babe, four dates and then a proposal."

Sadie went hot and cold, her body so sensitive she tingled all over. "You scare me half to death."

"You're not scared, you're excited, and that's a good feeling. It means your heart's beating, your blood's pumping, you are completely alive."

"It's a lot of adrenaline."

"Welcome to the world of a bull rider." He gave her a wink, his expression smug, but also playful and she didn't know what to do with him, she really didn't.

He was simply more of everything.

More handsome. More rugged. More interesting. More determined. More persuasive. More seductive.

And the destructive side... that seemed to be going, if not gone.

It didn't make sense.

"What's the matter now?" he asked, closing the distance and kissing her, a sizzling electric kiss that made her feel as if he was branding her his.

"Nothing."

"Then let's discuss it tomorrow. I want to take you ice-skating. I was thinking I'd pick you up around lunch, and we could get a bite to eat and then head up to Miracle Lake.

Trey and Mac are taking the kids skating, too, and McKenna would love for you to join us."

"She knows we're spending time together?"

"I stopped by the house earlier and filled her in a little."

"Filled her in on what?"

"That I'm going to be here through Christmas, and you and I are spending time together."

"And what did she say to that?"

"She suggested I bring you home for dinner tomorrow night after we're done skating."

"Rory, you know I have plans tomorrow evening."

"Yes, I do, but she didn't, and we're talking about an afternoon skating event. I can take you home in plenty of time so you can get ready for your date with Paul."

She ignored the date-with-Paul comment. "Well, do thank her for me. Ordinarily, I'd love to have dinner at her house."

"Just thank her when we skate."

"I'm not skating. I can't. I need to work."

"You are so full of excuses."

"Want to come over and see what I need to do? I have orders stacking up."

"Sure. What time should I be there?"

Sadie groaned because she knew he meant it, too. He would be there. She had no doubt about it. "No. You can't come over. I wouldn't get anything done."

"I'm really good with my hands."

Her pulse jumped, and everything inside her jumped, too. It was all she could do not to glance at his hands, and imagine his hands on her.

"I don't doubt it," she said feeling breathless, "but I won't be able to focus with you there. You're a huge distraction."

"So work in the morning and then come out after lunch."

"Rory, I'm a terrible ice skater, and I mean *terrible*. I'm one of those people whose ankles go in, and I stagger across the ice because I take choppy little steps because I don't know how to glide and then someone comes close, and I fling my arms out and lose my balance anyway and end up spread-eagled."

He grinned. "I can't decide if that's wonderful or awful."

"It's awful. Trust me. Skate, wobble, fall. Skate, wobble, fall. You'd be so embarrassed to be seen with me."

"You forget I've spent the past twenty-five years getting tossed on my butt, if not by a bronc, then by a bull."

"Yes, but that's because they're *bucking*. When I'm skating it's just me and the ice and the ice isn't moving."

"Practice makes perfect."

"Maybe, when I can afford a broken arm or leg." She reached out and gave his bicep a light squeeze, and then squeezed it again when she felt the delightfully hard, carved muscle. "Nice guns, bud."

His husky laugh sent another ripple of pleasure through

her and Sadie had to tell herself to be careful, and take it easy, because she was falling for him, the real him, hard and fast.

"Make tomorrow family time," she said, pulling her hand away. "You haven't seen a lot of McKenna and her kids, and I'm sure TJ is dying to show you some of his moves. Apparently, he's one of the best young hockey players in Marietta."

"Mac said the same thing to me today. I'm looking forward to seeing him on the ice."

"Have fun."

"I will, and we'll be sure to see each other soon."

WE'LL HAVE TO *see each other soon* did not mean, at Grey's Saloon, Sunday night while she was out with Paul.

But there he was, walking into Grey's with Trey and Troy Sheenan five minutes before the big Sunday night game.

Sadie's first instinct was to slide under the table and then her next was indignation. What was Rory doing here tonight? He knew she was meeting Paul to watch the game tonight. Did he really have to come to Grey's tonight, too?

For the first thirty minutes of the game, she managed to ignore Rory and the Sheenan twins as they settled at an open table over in the corner, drinking their beer and eating burgers—and okay, she did glance over a couple times, but they were just quick glances and she never made eye contact with Rory, nor would she. But the fact that she was sneaking glances over annoyed her, so she shifted her chair towards Paul's, ensuring that Rory's table was no longer in her line of sight.

Paul was delighted by her move, and reaching out, he pulled her chair even closer so that they were now side by side. And once they were that close, he reached for her hand, holding it under the table.

Sunday night football was going from bad to worse. Sadie had held Paul's hand before, and while there had never been sparks, she hadn't minded his touch. Tonight, however, she felt completely different and completely uncomfortable. There was nothing even remotely pleasant about holding hands… his palm felt moist, his fingers felt thick, his hold too firm.

She told herself the only reason she was uncomfortable was because Rory was here. She also told herself she couldn't let Rory be such a big influence yet. It wasn't as if she and Rory were exclusive, either.

"I can order you something besides the beer," Paul said, leaning towards her, moving in so close she wondered if he was going to try to kiss her. They'd kissed, too, brief, heatless kisses that she spent trying to think of something else. Clearly, Paul was not the right one for her.

"Why?" she asked.

"You've barely touched your beer."

"I'm good. Just trying to take it slow. We have three full quarters ahead of us."

"You're not driving tonight. I'll be sure to get you home safely."

She smiled at him unable to think of an answer to that. Because of course he'd get her home safely. Everything he did was safe and slow, and conscientious. "But on second thought, if you want to order me something, I'd love a water."

"And some more wings?"

"Perfect." Sadie eased her damp hand from his. "I'm just going to head to the ladies' room. I'll be right back."

In the bathroom, Sadie paced the small floor, back and forth, fighting panic and frustration. What was she doing here with Paul? Why had she continued dating him when she'd never felt any spark or true connection? Or had she thought Paul was suitable before Rory came home and turned her world on its head?

She wouldn't be surprised if Rory was the problem here. She appreciated his determination and drive. It had made him successful. But he couldn't steamroll right over her. He wasn't going to push her around. If she wanted to date other people, she would. And if she wanted to only date Rory, she would. It wasn't his call. He couldn't make that decision for her. Rory was no saint. He had to have dated dozens, if not hundreds, of buckle bunnies and she'd never judged him.

Leaving the restroom, she had a feeling she'd find Rory

in the hall, waiting for her. But he wasn't there, and she felt a little deflated as she passed the pool tables in the back and headed towards her table. And then she saw him, seated in her chair at her table, talking to Paul.

Sadie couldn't believe it. She froze for a moment, just taking it in. What was he doing talking to Paul?

Rory rose as she reached the table. He gave her his devastatingly sexy smile as he leaned across to give her a hug and then a kiss on the cheek.

"Good to see you here," he said, his hand lingering on her back, his palm warm, the pressure firm.

She managed a smile. "What are you doing here?"

"I came to watch the game." He gestured to his table with Trey and Troy. "Thought it would be good to get out of the house a little bit, give the women some freedom."

She wasn't buying it. "You mean, leave the women home alone with the kids while you guys go out and play?"

"Actually, the kids have babysitters. McKenna is in her photography studio developing prints, and Taylor is in Bozeman doing some Christmas shopping." He gave her a look as if daring her to add something.

She wouldn't take the bait.

Paul was oblivious to any tension. He turned to Rory. "Join us. We can pull up another chair."

Rory shook his head. "Thanks, but I better get back. I just wanted to say hello, and introduce myself."

"Good of you, Rory," Paul said earnestly, shaking Rory's

hand. "Nice to meet you, especially as I've heard so much about you over the years."

Rory returned to his table without a single glance back at Sadie. And Sadie knew he didn't look at her because she watched him all the way.

But five minutes later her phone vibrated, alerting her to a new text. She pulled her phone from her purse and checked the message.

It was from a number she didn't recognize, but the message cleared up any confusion as to who the sender was.

"He's a nice guy, babe, but he's not for you."

She lifted her head, looked over to Rory's table and he was looking at her.

Sadie ground her teeth in frustration, quickly texting back. *"How did you get my number?"*

"McKenna."

"You're interrupting my date."

"You're letting me interrupt."

She shot him another dark look before turning her phone off and putting it back in her purse.

It wasn't until she got home that night and turned her phone back on that she saw he'd sent her one last message.

"I'm going to be at Miracle Lake tomorrow morning at nine. I know you don't go into work until noon. Don't be a coward. Come meet me. I know you want to."

CHAPTER EIGHT

SHE WAS THERE at Miracle Lake at nine on the dot. Rory was already there at the clearing, leaning against his truck.

"You don't need to look so smug," she said, stepping from her car and slamming the door shut behind her.

He grinned, a lazy, self-satisfied smile that made it clear he never once doubted that she wouldn't show up. "You look beautiful."

"I'm wearing jeans and my marshmallow coat. I don't look beautiful."

"I happen to really like marshmallows."

She gave him a quelling glance, and she walked with him to the hut that rented the skates. "Tell me, why are we doing this?"

"It's good to get you out of your comfort zone."

"News flash, Douglas, you are out of my comfort zone."

He laughed and gave her a little hug. "You're a tad grumpy today, Mann. What's gotten into you?"

"If you'd asked me to breakfast, I'd be delighted, especially if I could order some pancakes. Or if you'd invited me to help you tackle your Christmas shopping that would have been great. But, skating? Not so much."

"How do you feel about snowboarding?"

"Have never been."

"Skiing?"

"Tried it a couple times but I hate the part where I lose control and go downhill too fast."

"You might like cross-country skiing then."

"Can we just stick with rides and drives? I really enjoy those things more."

His lips twitched. "Do movies meet with your approval?"

"Yes."

"Good. Because I've bought tickets for a movie Wednesday night. The Palace Theater is doing classics all December—"

"I know!" She did a little bounce as she faced him. "And this week is Holiday Inn. Is that the one we're seeing?"

"It is."

"It's a musical." She shot him a doubtful glance. "Did you know that?"

"Yes."

"That means there will be lots of singing and dancing."

"If you're hoping it's out of *my* comfort zone, you'll be disappointed. I like the classic movies, even the musicals."

He paid for their skate rentals and they carried them to a bench next to the frozen lake and put them on.

"Are you sure you can do this?" she asked tying the first

laces. "Skate two days in a row with that achy old hip of yours?"

"Sweetheart, you'd be amazed at what I can do with this achy old hip of mine."

She blushed hotly. "Why do you go there?"

"I don't." He laughed. "You do."

She didn't reply, concentrating on her second skate instead.

"So how was last night?" Rory asked, leaning against the bench, his skates already laced.

"Fine. Seahawks lost."

"That's disappointing."

She suspected there was a double meaning somewhere in his reply. She shrugged and carefully double knotted the laces. "The Seahawks' defense is hurting. We're definitely not the same team without the Legion of Boom."

"You know your football."

"Just Seattle." She sat up and pulled her gloves back on. "The pilot I dated was a huge Seahawks fan. He took me to a couple games. That was fun."

"Was he as nice as Paul?"

She rose and gave Rory a sweet smile. "No, Paul is nicer."

"That's good. You deserve a really nice guy."

And yet the way Rory said it managed to make *nice* sound like *boring*.

"I quite liked Paul," Rory added, getting to his feet.

"He's exactly the kind of person you'd want working for the city."

"Did you ask me to come here this morning so we could discuss my date, or did we come to skate?"

"We came to skate."

"Great." She took a wobbly step towards the rink. "Then let's get this over with, cowboy."

They slowly skated around the perimeter of the rink, their speed and caution that of two frail senior citizens than a pair still in their thirties. Fortunately, the ice was virtually empty since everyone was either at work or in school.

"I've never been here in winter and seen it so empty," she said.

"It's nice like this. Peaceful."

"I'd feel a little more peaceful if I wasn't afraid I'd fall any minute."

"It was definitely more fun before I was hurt." His smile was rueful. "But it feels good to be out here. I used to come a lot as a kid. We all did. Quinn was a great skater."

"Heard he was a nationally ranked hockey player at one point."

Rory nodded. "Growing up, Quinn played every sport and then gradually narrowed it down to hockey and baseball, and he had the chance to be drafted for both, but in the end went with baseball. I think he made a good choice. He's had a solid career, even if it's starting to wind down."

"So how did TJ look yesterday? Did he remind you of a

young Quinn?"

"He's got Quinn's natural athletic ability, but in looks, he's all Sheenan. He really is a mini Trey."

"Do you see Quinn often?"

"We met up last January before I returned to the circuit, and then I happened to be in Phoenix in March and was able to see him play a game during spring training."

"How much longer do you think he'll be playing baseball?"

"This might be his last season. He's ready to move on and do different things."

"Will he come back to Marietta?"

"He has a big house overlooking the Yellowstone River, but I don't think he's been there more than a couple times, and he's thinking about putting in on the market. I told him it could be a good rental and so he's asked me to take a look. I'm heading there after we finish here. Want to drive over with me?"

"I have to be at work at noon."

"I can have you back."

"Does that mean we get to stop skating soon?"

"Do you hate it that much?"

"No," she answered, apparently unconvincingly because Rory laughed.

They made another cautious loop around the rink, the sun glittering on the snow, and the only sound the scrape of their blades against the ice. Sadie drew in a deep breath, the frosty morning invigorating, the air smelling of pine. She wouldn't say she was comfortable, but as they finished their fourth sweeping circle, she did feel rather victorious for not falling once.

"How about we return the skates and head over to Quinn's house?" Rory suggested.

Sadie was delighted to call it a day, and once she'd changed back into her shoes, she went to the car and retrieved the small picnic basket she'd packed earlier with a thermos of hot coffee and cherry scones she'd baked that morning.

"Snacks for the road," she said, as Rory opened the passenger door of his truck for her and she climbed in.

"What do you have?"

"Coffee and scones."

"Sounds delicious, but should we wait for Quinn's? Don't want to risk getting you burned."

"Good plan."

Quinn's house was only another five minutes from the lake. It was a big, sprawling wood and stone house, one of those gorgeous mountain homes you'd see in a luxury magazine.

"Nice," she said.

"It is," he agreed, and yet she noted that when he parked, he faced the river instead of the imposing house. "Would you mind having coffee in the car? I rather like this view."

"Don't mind at all," she answered, placing the basket

between them and taking out two glazed mugs featuring green Christmas trees against a cheery red background. Sadie filled the mugs with coffee and then offered him one of the scones.

She watched as he bit into the scone and then smiled when he gave her a thumb's up.

"Delicious," he added.

"My mom's recipe. It's super easy, and since I had a little time earlier while the varnish was drying, thought I'd whip up a batch."

"They remind me of my mom's scones. She made hers with raisins or dried cranberries."

"You can make these with any kind of fruit. At Christmas my mom would use three kinds of berries and then drizzle a little icing on top."

"What else did she make for you?"

"Everything. She was very hands on. She made my clothes and cooked all our meals every day. We rarely ate out—it was expensive—but she also liked being home in the evening after being out working all day."

"How many days a week did she work?"

"Six. Sunday was her rest day."

"And where did you go on Saturdays?"

"When I was little, I'd go with her, and then when I was old enough to stay home alone, I did."

"You didn't have any aunts or uncles or grandparents nearby?"

"My parents moved here from Nebraska. My dad grew up in foster care and my mom grew up with an abusive dad and an alcoholic mom. I think they just wanted to escape their past and start fresh."

"And then your mom was widowed young."

"Yeah." Sadie unscrewed the coffee thermos and topped off his cup. "Because I never knew my dad she'd tell me little things about him. He was a redhead, like me, and he was really funny. Mom met him at a restaurant. She was the hostess, and he came in with some friends. She said the first thing she noticed was that he was handsome, but she didn't trust a really good looking man, and then he made her laugh, and that's when she fell in love. Mom said Dad made her laugh every single day."

Rory reached out and tucked one of her red strands behind her ear. "I wish I could have met them."

Sadie looked at him, her gaze meeting his and holding. "Do you mean that?"

"I do."

She leaned across the picnic basket and kissed him, slowly, sweetly, savoring the feel of his lips against hers. She reached up to lightly trail her fingernails down his cheek, feeling the contour of his cheekbone and then the angle of his jaw. He was such a hard man on the outside and yet so tender on the inside.

The kiss gradually deepened and then somehow she was on his lap, and the kiss was no longer slow or tender but full of hunger and heat. She wrapped her arms around his neck, her breasts pressed against his chest, her hips cradled by his hard thighs.

She thought she could kiss him forever. His kisses were that good. She loved everything about him… his smell, his taste, his warmth. He felt beautiful and exciting but also familiar. She'd been close to men before, but no one had ever made her feel this good. Being in his arms was the most natural place to be. When his hand slid up her hip, and over her waist she arched against him, wanting more.

"Angel girl, I could get lost in you," he said hoarsely.

She smiled against his mouth. "I was just thinking the same thing."

"But I won't get lost in you until you agree to be mine."

Sadie drew back, blinking, and stared into his intensely blue eyes. "*What?*"

"Not going to let the physical get out of hand until you marry me." He clasped her jaw and pressed another hot, hard, hungry kiss against her mouth, the pressure and heat lighting a fire in her veins.

It was a kiss that made her clutch his shirt and hang on, aching, breathless.

And then he did it again, and she couldn't even think clearly, head spinning, body melting, no defenses left. "You didn't make your other girlfriends wait," she said huskily.

"I didn't want to keep them. I want to keep you. And when we make our baby, we're going to be married. We're going to do this the way our parents would have wanted it done. In a church, with our family and friends there—"

"I haven't even said yes."

"But you will." He stroked his thumb over the fullness of her lower lip, making it tingle. "You want me as much as I want you."

"Sex isn't the basis for a relationship."

"Exactly. Which is why we're dating." He smiled into her eyes, his blue irises fierce and bright. "Two dates down. Two to go. And on the fourth date, I'm proposing."

"You're crazy."

"Which makes me perfect for you."

She laughed, a faintly hysterical bubble of sound. "You've only been in town three days. It doesn't work that way."

"In my world, it only takes eight seconds—"

"We are talking about bull riding."

"For an angel, you have one dirty mind." He gave her a light smack on her butt. "Now look at that house behind us. Do you like it?"

She looked over his shoulder, out the back window of the truck, and as she peeked over his shoulder she shifted her weight, deliberately rocking on the hard length of him, taking pleasure in his muffled groan. Serves him right. "It's fine."

"Why don't you like it?"

"It's too much. It reminds me of a hotel not a home."

"Do you prefer older homes, like the big Victorians on Bramble?"

"Why are you asking?"

"I'm trying to figure out what kind of house we'll buy when we're married."

Sadie leaned back, trying to block out the lovely pressure of him between her thighs. "Are we house hunting?"

"Not yet. But we will. We'll need a place of our own where we can raise our kids. I'm thinking a couple acres would be nice, but I don't need a lot of land."

"Are we really having this conversation?"

"Yes. Christmas is coming. With you on Clomid, you'll soon be in ovulation."

She clapped her hand over his mouth. "Not another word." She choked, mortified. "Please don't mention ovulation again."

"You're the one who asked if I'd show up at your Dr. Crookshank's with a plastic cup," he said, taking great pains to enunciate against her palm.

"That's different. It was a hypothetical question." Frowning, she drew her hand away. "Cowboy, things are moving really fast."

"Would it reassure you at all if I told you that McKenna thinks we're perfect for each other?"

"No."

"She said we're destined to be together—"

"No." Sadie pushed a heavy wave of hair back from her

face. "*No.*"

"Why?"

"Because…" Her voice faded.

She couldn't answer. She didn't have an answer. She just knew she was afraid and overwhelmed again, and she climbed off Rory's lap and settled in her seat, drawing the seatbelt across her lap and giving it a secure click.

Rory didn't speak, nor did he start the truck. They sat in silence facing the tumbling Yellowstone River. She kept hoping he'd say something eventually but he didn't, and after a while, the silence was too much to take.

She shifted uncomfortably, adjusting the seatbelt on her lap. "You asked me yesterday if I'd ever been in love, and I said once. I told you that I never told him." She rubbed her knuckles across her lips, nervous, upset. "The person I loved was you," she added after a moment. "But I don't know what that even meant, to say I loved you. I didn't know you. I saw you. I watched you. I read about you. But I didn't know you, and now you're here, and you're interested in me, and it's like an answer to prayer, but I'm suddenly not sure I understood what I was praying for."

She was still staring out at the river, but she knew he was looking at her. She could feel his gaze burning into her. He wasn't happy. She didn't blame him. It was a terrible thing to admit, but she had to be honest. She had to make him understand what she was thinking and feeling.

"Maybe I wasn't praying for you because I loved you, but

because I felt guilty," she added faintly, her mouth going dry because her heart was pounding so hard.

Rory sat utterly, perfectly still and part of her wondered what he was thinking, while another part just wanted him to start the truck and drive.

"Why would you feel guilty?" he asked after an endless, miserable silence.

"Because of what happened to your family," she said, trying not to shrivel on the inside.

"But why would that make you feel guilty? You weren't in any way responsible."

She wanted then to tell him everything, about how McKenna had been at her house, at her birthday, when her family had been killed.

She wanted to tell him how she remembered every little thing from that night. It had been a beautiful, August evening, the sunlight lingering as it did in Montana in the summer. Sadie had been beyond excited to have the popular girls coming to her house for the sleepover, and how if it weren't for McKenna saying yes at the last minute, the others wouldn't have come.

She wanted to tell him how McKenna was one of the first to arrive and Sadie was standing on her front porch as Rory pulled up to the house in his old truck. The long rays of golden light gilded him as he drew to a stop. He turned his head towards McKenna and said something that made her laugh, and then McKenna climbed out of the truck with her sleeping bag, pillow, and the present. McKenna answered Rory, making him laugh.

Sadie never forgot that sliver of time. Rory so handsome at the wheel, pulling away from the curb a little too fast, his country music a little too loud, and pretty, smiling McKenna walking up the sidewalk with her things for the sleepover.

It was without a doubt, the biggest moment of Sadie's life. But the party didn't go as planned. Just hours later two sheriff cars arrived to pick McKenna up, lights flashing, sirens blaring. All the girls had rushed to the window, watching as the officers spoke to Mrs. Mann outside, and then Mrs. Mann came inside and drew McKenna away from the others, walking her out to where the officers waited.

It was only after the patrol cars had gone that Mrs. Mann told Sadie there had been a tragedy at the Douglas Ranch. Sadie started crying and couldn't stop. The girls called their parents and went home.

"I don't understand the guilt," Rory said now, his voice hard, almost harsh. "And why me, why not Quinn?"

She opened her mouth to speak but no sound came out. Her stomach cramped, her insides knotting with pain.

"I don't know," she finally whispered. "It was just always you."

He said nothing for a minute, and then he started the truck and drove her back to Miracle Lake. He pulled up next to her car and shifted into park.

They hadn't said a word since leaving Quinn's house,

and Sadie's hands shook as she lifted the picnic basket. "Thank you," she said, opening the truck door.

He turned and looked at her, his blue gaze burning into her. "For what, angel?"

"Being… understanding."

His gaze slowly raked her, from the top of her head to her fleece-lined boots. "I'll see you Wednesday. The movie starts at seven thirty. Let's get dinner first."

"You still want to go?"

"We made a deal. Two more dates, darlin'."

RORY WAITED FOR Sadie to start her car and get safely on the road before he left, but once he was driving he didn't know where to go, nor did he know what to do with himself. Coming home was beyond uncomfortable. Coming home created pain, real pain, serious pain, the kind that couldn't be eased with three ibuprofin tablets and a tall glass of water.

He'd known when he drove up to the ranch Saturday afternoon that he had work to do. He'd accepted that it was time to deal with who he'd become, and with what he'd never had. Love. Marriage. Family.

Years ago he'd convinced himself he didn't deserve love.

Years ago he'd convinced himself he wasn't responsible enough, good enough, strong enough…

But somehow in the past few days, he'd come to realize he didn't have to be perfect. He wasn't supposed to be perfect. He wasn't God. He was just a man.

Rory turned off the highway and traveled down the road that led to the Marietta cemetery. The big iron gates were open, and he drove past the groundskeeper cottage and then on past the chapel, trying to remember where the five graves would be. He hadn't been back to the cemetery since the funeral. He wasn't even sure why he was here now, only that he felt compelled to stop and pay his respects.

He drove slowly around the perimeter trying to remember something from that day. It had been summer. And hot. There had been shade. But was that from the canopy or a tree?

He braked and called McKenna before he could change his mind.

She answered almost right away.

He cleared his throat. "Mac, it's me. I'm over at the cemetery, but I can't find where they, um, all are. Can you help me?"

She hesitated only a moment. "They are in the far right corner about four rows in if you were walking towards the middle."

He was grateful she sounded so matter of fact. "Thanks, Mac."

"Of course."

And then they hung up, and Rory took his foot off the brake and then continued around the perimeter, heading for the far right corner. Once there, he parked, and stepped out of the truck and made his way over four rows and then began reading the gravestones, paying attention to the names and dates and it was overwhelming. All these people, all loved.

He had to stop a couple of times and look up and breathe while he focused on Copper Mountain's snow-capped peak.

He wanted to turn around and return to his truck and get out of here. This was a bad idea—

And then he saw Gordon's gravestone, and he froze. Ah, little Gordon.

Rory closed his eyes, drawing air into his lungs, trying to ease the fire and then he knelt down and put his hand on Gordon's name, and said a prayer for him.

He did this for each of them. Prayed for them, and silently told them he loved them. When he finished, he was grateful for his cane as he stiffly pushed to his feet.

He turned around to start back to his truck and stopped. Just a few feet away stood McKenna.

"What are you doing here?" he said gruffly.

"Came to make sure my big brother was okay."

"I'm okay."

She went to him then and wrapped her arms around him, giving him a hard hug.

He hugged her back.

"Love you, Rory," she whispered.

"Love you, too, Mac. Just sorry I haven't been around more."

"You're allowed to live your own life. In fact, you're supposed to live your own life." She smiled up at him. "You were never meant to stay here and cluck over us like a mother hen."

"I hate that I've worried you."

"Rory, you're here. You're well. Best of all, you're home for Christmas. What more can I ask?"

He turned away, looked back at the bare gray gravestones. "Do you ever come here? Do you ever talk to them?"

"I usually come on each of their birthdays with flowers."

"This is the first time I've come since the funeral."

"I wondered."

"Is that terrible?"

"No. We can't live in the past. No point in that."

CHAPTER NINE

SADIE SPENT THE rest of the day hoping he'd call.

She needed him to call so she could apologize. She needed him to call so she could tell him she was confused and what she'd said to him was true, but at the same time, it was only a partial truth.

The whole truth was that she didn't understand why she'd decided all those years ago that Rory was the one for her.

She didn't understand how she could feel so strongly for him, and only him, for years on end.

She didn't understand why her heart had chosen him and then refused to let go… and then right when she let go, he showed up, and he was a million times bigger and more thrilling then the man she'd followed from afar.

She didn't understand how love worked, and she didn't understand what made her feelings for him so intense. And they were intense. Yes, there was some guilt, but there was also tenderness, protectiveness, admiration, respect, and desire. So much desire. He was beautiful, and male, and her ideal as men went. She couldn't imagine ever being this attracted to anyone else.

And that was what frightened her the most. If he was the only one for her, how would she cope when he wasn't there?

If he walked away from her, what would she do?

She paced her house, moving from the living room through the dining room to the compact kitchen and then out again to look towards the bedrooms. Her room and her mom's room. After moving back into the house Sadie had taken her old room. She couldn't imagine ever wanting her mom's room, even if it was bigger.

Truthfully, this wasn't her forever house. She didn't want to raise her children here. She wanted a fresh start.

Sadie suddenly thought of Rory and she pictured him today at the ice rink, and then again sitting in the truck outside Quinn's house. She didn't need a fancy house. All she really wanted was Rory there.

Sadie glanced at her phone, checking the time, checking for missed calls, checking for text messages.

It was eight, and there was nothing.

Her heart hurt. She hurt. And she wondered if he hurt.

She'd said it all wrong earlier. She'd been wrong. Now she desperately wanted to make it right.

She could call him. Or text. Or wait and hope he'd call her tomorrow.

But she would never sleep tonight, not when she felt so upset.

Sadie shoved her feet into her winter boots and pulled on

her heavy coat and jumped into her car and drove the four short blocks to Rory's stable-house. The house looked dark except for the porch lights that were on.

She went to the door anyway, and rang the bell. *Let him be home, let him be home, let him—*

The door swung open and he was there, barefoot in jeans and an open flannel shirt.

She sucked in a breath and stared at his beautifully muscled chest and then down lower to the hard carved knots of his abdominal muscles. This wasn't a six pack. It was an eight pack. Or more.

"Ahem. My eyes are up here," he drawled, mouth curved in a faint dry smile.

She jerked her head up, heat and need rushing through her, heightening her emotions. "Forgive me." She breathed. "Rory, I said things this morning I didn't mean. I panicked about... everything... and, yes, I do feel guilty that—"

"I think you better come in," he said, opening the door wider. "Sounds like this might take awhile."

"I don't want to barge in. I just want you to know that I am sorry. I'm sorry I don't know how to do this with you."

"Are you breaking up with me, darlin'?"

"No."

"Then come in, because I'm freezing."

She followed him into the little house, watching nervously as he shut the door and then headed into the kitchen. "I just opened a bottle of red," he said, gesturing to the bottle

151

and glass on the island. "Want to join me?"

She nodded. "Yes. Please."

He poured her a glass and handed it to her. "You drink this. I'm going to get something warmer to put on."

He returned a minute later with, the flannel shirt replaced by a t-shirt and a v-neck cashmere sweater and sheepskin slippers on his feet. "So," he said, drawing out a barstool and sitting down. "What's happening?"

"Today at Quinn's house I said things that I thought I meant, but maybe I meant some of it, but not all of it." She frowned, forehead wrinkling. "I'm sure that confuses you because it confuses me."

"What did you say that you didn't mean?"

"I didn't pray for you all these years because I felt guilty. I prayed for you because I care for you."

"Guilt is such a strong word."

"It is. And guilt is such a heavy thing. But it's not what makes me want to be around you. *You* make me want to be around you. I love the way you enter a room. You walk like a rock star and it makes me smile, every single time. And then I love the way you smile… it's so sexy and confident and the fact that you are so sexy and confident drives me mad because I've never felt that way once in my life." She took a quick breath. "I love your eyes. They are so blue. And when you smile, your eyes smile, and you get these little creases here." She reached out and gently touched the corner of his eye.

"And I love the way you kiss me," she added after a moment. "And the way you tease me. You make me laugh, and when I'm not panicking, you really make me happy."

He looked into her eyes for a long moment. "Why do you panic?"

"Because I'm afraid of having the very thing I always dreamed of."

He didn't blink. His gaze never wavered. "Maybe I'm not it… him… the dream. Maybe I'm just the place holder until you meet the one. The right one."

His words felt like a knife in her heart. She exhaled slowly, trying to manage the pain. "I wouldn't be here now if I didn't think you might be… the one. I wouldn't have made myself sick today if I didn't genuinely care."

"I don't doubt that you care. But that doesn't mean we're necessarily right for each other. Maybe we did get ahead of ourselves. Maybe this is a good time to take a step back. As you said, you have options. You have your donors—"

She kissed him to stop his words. She couldn't bear to listen another moment longer. His mouth was firm and cool. He didn't try to kiss her back.

Her eyes burned, but she wouldn't give up. Lightly she stroked his cheek, and then the line of his jaw. "I waited forever for you to come home," she whispered. "Please don't give up on me so soon."

His hand clasped the back of her head, holding her still,

while he kissed her deeply, fiercely, kissing her as though her mouth and her body and soul belonged to him. She was trembling by the time he lifted his head, and she had to lean against him, heart hammering, legs unsteady.

"Take it easy, sweetheart." He ran his hand through her thick hair, pushing it back from her face. "Haven't given up. Not even close."

"Even though it's been one tumultuous ride?"

He smiled his lazy, daredevil smile. "That's my favorite kind," he said, before kissing her for a long, long time.

RORY WORKED OUT Tuesday morning and then went to breakfast at the diner and after breakfast he entered Risa's flower shop, ordering flowers to be delivered to Sadie at Marietta Properties this afternoon.

He held the pen over the small cream florist card, trying to think of something appropriate to say. He hadn't sent flowers to a woman since... well ever. No, not true. He'd sent flowers to McKenna after the birth of each of her babies. But that didn't count. Sending his sister flowers wasn't the same as sending his love interest flowers, especially after a bumpy day.

What did you say on a card the size of matchbook? There wasn't room for anything. Rory frowned, and tapped the pen against the counter, aware that the florist was waiting, patiently. Finally he scrawled, *Not from Paul.* And then slipped the card in the envelope and handed it to the woman.

SADIE WAS AT her desk when the huge vase of red roses, white freesias, tulips, and miniature candy canes arrived. It was a massive arrangement, requiring her to shift her computer monitor over so the arrangement could have a huge chunk of her desk.

Natalie emerged from her office. "Wow. That's some serious love. Who is it from?"

"I don't know." Sadie searched in the red and white blossoms for a card, and finally found it attached to a candy cane. She opened the sealed envelope and drew out the stiff ivory card. *Not from Paul.*

Sadie smiled, and couldn't stop smiling.

He was awful, and wonderful. Arrogant, confident, strong, patient, forgiving.

"Stop grinning like the Cheshire Cat," Natalie said. "Who sent them?"

"Rory," Sadie said, slipping the card back in the envelope.

"What did he say to make you smile like that?"

"*Not from Paul.*"

"I don't get it."

"It's an inside joke."

"How is that romantic?"

Her lips lifted. "It's not, but that's what makes it kind of perfect."

WEDNESDAY NIGHT, SADIE met Rory downtown at the Chinese restaurant next door to the movie theater. He'd offered to pick her up, but she told him she needed to go check on one of the rental properties and make sure the cleaning crew had come as new guests were arriving tomorrow.

He accepted her explanation and yet she felt a twinge of guilt, and she really didn't want or need to feel more guilt, not when it came to Rory. The guilt was oppressive and it wasn't fair. She hadn't done anything wrong. Nothing bad had taken place at her house, and yet her party had been ruined, and Sadie had never liked celebrating her birthday afterwards because her birthday was the anniversary of the Douglas Ranch murders. And every year on her birthday, the newspapers would have a story somewhere on the front page, or another prominent page about the unsolved murders of the Douglas family.

Sadie pushed away the memories and entered the restaurant, checking to see if Rory had already arrived. While she spoke to the hostess, the front door opened and Rory entered, looking every bit as handsome as a movie star.

Everything seemed to light up inside of her as he walked towards her, and she smiled a wide, bright smile, unable to hide her happiness.

She was crazy about him.

"Hello, angel girl," he said, leaning down to kiss her cheek.

She lifted her face and he kissed her lips.

"I loved my flowers," she said, still smiling, and feeling as if it was Christmas. "Thank you so much."

"My pleasure."

They were seated at a cozy corner table and immediately served hot tea which was the perfect way to start the meal on such a chilly night.

Sadie couldn't remember the last time she had Chinese food, and she certainly couldn't remember when it tasted this good. Admittedly, Chinese food in Marietta Montana wasn't very authentic, but everything was delicious. The potstickers were golden and firm on the outside and tender on the inside. The chow mein was full of tender bites of chicken and pork and shrimp. Best of all, Rory was great company. They talked about nothing and everything, the hour passing so quickly that they had to rush out of the restaurant with their fortune cookies in their hand to make the seven thirty showing of the film.

"I hope they still have seats," he said.

"It's a big theater," she answered.

After all that rushing, they laughed as they entered the auditorium and discovered it nearly empty.

"Maybe they're still trying to park," she said.

"Or maybe they're stuck in traffic."

"Because Marietta has so much traffic," she teased, as they found seats in the middle of the auditorium.

Minutes later the theater darkened and a half dozen previews played before the film began.

Rory took her hand as the opening scene of *Holiday Inn* unfolded, and she felt a bubble of warmth fill her chest. Her hand belonged in his. She belonged with him. For the first time in forever, everything felt right in her world. And even though her mom was gone, Sadie couldn't help but think that if her mother knew Rory, the real Rory, she'd approve of him. It was just a shame she died without ever knowing how wonderful Rory Douglas really was.

"You're quiet," Rory said, as they slowly left the theater, arm in arm.

"Just thinking about Mom, and how we always watched the Christmas movies together. We loved the classics. We would watch as many as we could every year. This one was one of our favorites."

"But it's made you sad."

"Not sad, just… a little wistful." She glanced up at him. "I wish my mom had met you. She heard me talk about you, but it's not the same thing. You're so much… more… than I even imagined."

"What did you imagine?"

"I don't know. That's the problem with fantasies. You're not dealing in reality. I never really knew you."

"So why did you like me?"

"Because you're handsome—that's very shallow, I realize—but it's true. And I fell for your smile early on. I remember it from high school. And you had this great shaggy head of hair, a dark dirty blonde that went perfect with your tan."

"I haven't heard anything yet about my intelligence, or my keen wit."

She gurgled with laughter. "You are funny."

"Thank you."

"And smart, and fascinating, and I've been fascinated by you forever."

"So if you liked me so much, why not come talk to me all those years ago? Why not introduce yourself?"

"I told you. I got scared. I psyched myself out."

"Not judging you, sweetheart, but I don't get it."

"I know, but you're a bull rider. You risk your life every night you compete. It's natural for you to race towards danger. I don't like danger."

"And yet you worked as a flight attendant for ten years."

"That was different. I wasn't flying the plane. I was just making sure the customers were comfortable and safe. See? Safety first. I'm actually massively risk adverse."

"I'm beginning to think that's why you never married. It's a risk."

"You're not wrong. Becoming a mom doesn't scare me as much as falling in love."

"Remember how you idealized me a little tiny bit?"

She blushed. "Yes, and your point is?"

"I'm concerned you're idealizing motherhood, too. It's not going to be easy being a parent."

"I know, but I'm ready for it, and maybe it's my age, and the ticking of the biological clock, but I'm ready for the rest of my life. I want everything that I waited for, everything that other women my age have."

"Such as?"

"Babies and diapers and play dates. Birthday cakes and parties and stockings and Christmas presents. I don't want to have a quiet little life. I want kids and noise and chaos. I want a cookie jar on my counter always full of freshly baked cookies and little people coming in and out to ask what's for dinner."

"That sounds wonderful, but you never mention a man."

They stood on the street corner facing each other.

"You always mention children," he added, "but you never say anything about having a husband to love, or a father for the kids."

"I don't mean it to sound that way. I guess I've learned to focus on the things I can control. I can't be a father, but I can be a great mother, and that's why years ago I decided to be that mom who volunteers for everything. I'm going to be as involved as I possibly can be... chaperoning field trips, organizing talent shows, sewing costumes for the Christmas pageant." She wrapped her scarf more snugly around her throat. "I actually can't wait to make sheep and camels and robes for the shepherds and wise men."

"So while you sew, what will your children's father do?"

She frowned, trying to imagine it. "I don't know. What did your dad do? What would *you* do?"

"I'd take the kids skating since their mom doesn't know how. I'd teach them how to throw a snowball—a critical skill every boy and girl needs. I'd get them sledding, since Mom again, is afraid of speed and losing control."

He was referring to her as the mom in this case and it sent a little shiver through her, a shiver that was part pleasure and part pain. "And what about husbands? What do they do?"

"Well, your husband would lug in the Christmas tree and get it stable in the stand. He'd chop firewood and carry it in. He'd get the ornament boxes down from the attic and then put on some Christmas music—maybe some Bing Crosby, Brad Paisley, or Michael Buble—and then he'd want to dance with you to one of the slow, tender songs—"

"He would not."

"He would, too, if it was me married to you."

Her heart did a quick mad double beat. "What else would he do?" she whispered.

"He'd make his famous eggnog—"

"Does he have a famous eggnog recipe?"

"Absolutely. The secret Douglas recipe. And then at night, he'd hold his sweetheart, thanking God and feeling mighty blessed."

It sounded wonderful, she thought, maybe too wonderful, because real life wasn't like that. She didn't trust the picture he painted, it sounded too much like one of those Norman Rockwell paintings that used to grace *Life* magazine. Sadie only knew about them because her mother would bring home dusty issues of the magazine from one of the houses she cleaned. The magazines were so old, and some of them smelled musty with age, but her mother kept them and would read them.

Sadie turned her face away from Rory and looked out at the street. She suddenly felt claustrophobic, and she tugged on her scarf now, trying to loosen the woven fabric.

"What's wrong?" he asked.

She shrugged dismissively. "It just sounds a bit too much like a fairytale."

"Which part?"

"I don't know... all of it?"

"Are you saying you don't believe in love?"

"I'm saying that love isn't all rainbows and moonbeams."

"And it's not unicorns and pots of gold, either," he answered. "But love is real, and marriage isn't always easy, but my parents were really happy together. My mom and dad were best friends. Even after five kids, they were best friends."

She didn't speak and Rory filled the silence. "Even when I was frustrated with my father, I still knew I was lucky to have him, not because he was this great provider—truthfully, we hurt for money and he was a lousy rancher—but he loved us, and he loved our mom. He didn't just tolerate her, or respect her, he absolutely adored her and there was nothing more important to him than being kind to her, and making sure we kids understood what an amazing woman we had as our mother."

Rory tilted her chin up and he looked down into her eyes. "Maybe that is why I believe the best scenario of all is a family with two parents, as there is no greater gift than two adults who love and respect each other, raising their children together."

"You're saying I couldn't be a good single mother?"

"I'm not saying that. I think you'd be amazing at whatever you set your mind to. But why go that route if you don't have to? Why choose that path when you could have a partner? Don't you want someone to love you? Because you deserve it. You deserve a man who will love you, and cherish you, a man who'll make you laugh and hug you when you're sad. You deserve a man who will be your best friend."

"Fairytales again," she said quietly.

"Believe me, it's not. And it's not unrealistic to want it, or think it could happen."

She held her breath, the icy air making her eyes water and her cheeks sting. Silence stretched, the quiet only broken by the passing of a car, tires crunching the salted road.

"I'm afraid," she whispered, "afraid to want too much

because then I'd risk disappointment."

"Is that why you only wanted me when I was on the circuit... far away... just a fantasy?"

She exhaled hard. "I want you now. You're just, you know, a lot more overwhelming in the flesh."

"And you haven't even seen all the flesh."

Sadie laughed and then punched him in the arm. "That one was you, all you. It's not my mind that's dirty, it's yours, Rory Douglas."

He laughed a low, husky laugh, and wrapped his arm around her, holding her close. "So you do want me."

He felt solid and warm, and he smelled so good, too, fresh and clean with a hint of spice. "Of course I do!" She let herself sink in to his embrace, feeling unbearably secure. "But I am scared," she admitted after a moment.

She couldn't look at him as she talked, and she toyed with the snaps on his sheepskin jacket. "I've never cared for anyone this much, and the more I feel, the more afraid I am that it won't last, and then what would I do? How would I survive? I don't want to be that lady crying every night in her room." She was horrified by her confession but also relieved to have said it.

She'd spent her life trying to be optimistic and hopeful but underneath she was afraid, aware that life was dangerous and unpredictable, and that love was often too fragile for the rigors of the world.

Her mom was one of the kindest, hardest working women Sadie knew. She never complained, and she never acted as if she couldn't cope with the pressures of life, and yet late at night when she thought Sadie was sleeping, she'd break down crying.

Sadie would sit next to her bedroom door, listening to her mom weeping in the next room. Her mom didn't cry every night, but she cried often enough that Sadie would try to take on more around the house, wanting to help, wanting to make things easier for her mom, but no matter how much Sadie pitched in, it was never enough.

Sadie struggled with her secret burden as she grew up. How was it possible that her mom, who was so hardworking and kind, could be the saddest person Sadie had ever met?

"You won't be that lady crying in her room every night because you're more resilient than that, Sadie." Rory's voice was hard, and no-nonsense. "If your heart gets broken, then you'll pick yourself up after a bit and carry on. Hearts do heal—"

"Not everyone's."

He fell silent.

"Not everyone survives a broken heart," she added lowly. "I'm not trying to be dramatic, either. It's just… I know firsthand."

"You mean your mom never got over your dad's death."

She nodded once, jaw tight.

"You aren't your mom, Sadie."

"She never complained but she was deeply unhappy."

"Again, you're not her. You can make different decisions. You can choose happiness."

CHAPTER TEN

THE NEXT AFTERNOON while Rory was doing a little Christmas shopping in town he got a call from a realtor based out of Denver asking about the Douglas Ranch.

Rory was immediately on guard. He'd had so many of these calls over the past two decades, calls from realtors and interested buyers that weren't serious about purchasing the property. Instead they were scouts for a paranormal TV show, and crime solvers, and amateur ghost hunters. Or they were prospective buyers who offered Rory pennies for the property, thinking he'd jump at the chance to dump the ranch.

Those people didn't understand what the Douglas Ranch meant to him, and the family. Yes, something awful had happened there twenty-two years ago, but before that night, it had been land that had been passed down from generation to generation. What he wanted for the property was to find a good buyer, someone who'd take care of it, and put up a handsome new house somewhere, maybe on one of those rolling hills with a view of the valley and the river below.

"It's been off the market for a number of years," Rory

said.

"Would you be open to receiving an offer?" the realtor asked.

"Is the buyer familiar with the ranch's history?"

"Yes."

Rory could hear the realtor shuffling some papers.

"He competed with you on the American Extreme Bull Rider Tour this past year," the realtor added. "You mentioned your property, and how it could be available if you found the right buyer."

"You're not going to tell me his name?"

"I'm just doing some legwork right now."

Rory felt the old tightness in his chest. It was still so hard to discuss the ranch with anyone. "What can I tell you?"

"The most recent appraisal I can find is five years old. Does that sound correct?"

"Yes."

Rory hated even discussing the ranch. "As you can see from the last appraisal, as well as comps of property in the area, it's good land."

"It needs improving."

"What land doesn't?"

"But it's sat vacant for twenty years, hasn't it?" the realtor answered.

"I'm not interested in a low-ball offer."

"It wouldn't be a low-ball offer."

"What does he want to do with it? Chop it up and turn

it into ranchettes?"

"No, he wants to run livestock on it."

"It seems to me the problem isn't whether or not I'd sell. The problem is whether or not he really wants to pull the trigger after he reads the full disclosure. That's been the issue virtually every time. It's not the appraisal, and it's not the bank. It's the buyer."

"The buyer is familiar with what occurred, and just to clarify, he doesn't need a bank. He has cash, it'd be close to a full offer, and he'd like to close quickly. Before Christmas if possible."

Rory was stunned. It was almost too good to be true. "There are no buildings on the property anymore. The house and barn were torn down. The area has been scraped clean. Only thing you'll find there now is snow, and come spring, wildflowers. They've pretty much taken over the place."

"That's perfect. He wants to build. And who doesn't like wildflowers?"

"I know you don't want to disclose your client's name yet, but if you're telling me he's serious, and he wants to put some love into that land, I guarantee we can make a fair deal, and close quickly. That property has stood empty too long. It's time for a new owner, and time for my family to move on."

"My client is thinking the same thing. I'll be in touch again soon."

Rory hung up and sat there in his chair, before his computer, staring into space. That was an incredible call. It'd be even more incredible if this mystery buyer made a respectable offer and they did close before the new year.

He was still lost in thought when his phone rang. He ignored the first couple of rings, and then when he finally glanced down and saw it was Sadie calling, he answered. "Afternoon."

"You okay?"

"Yes."

"Good." She hesitated. "So, I was calling to see if you'd want to do something with me. You've planned all these dates and I thought maybe it was my time to plan something for us. It'd be early next week."

"Sounds good."

"Are you free?"

He laughed, picturing his calendar. It was virtually wide open. "Yes. What are we doing, or is it a surprise?"

"It's called Mistletoe and Montana. It's an annual Christmas tree auction usually held in Livingston, but it's been moved to Marietta this year, and it's going to be at the Graff. I was just offered two pairs of tickets—it's a fancy evening event—if I'd be willing to help out with one of the trees and I thought if I'd ask you, and if you said yes, then McKenna and Trey, too."

"What do you have to do for these four tickets?"

"Design a themed tree."

"Just design it?"

She hesitated. "Decorate it, too." When he said nothing she hurriedly added, "They lost one of their sponsors or something, and they're in a bind and I know it's going to be a lot of work but I think it could be a good way to get my name out there and I love things like this. I love to be creative."

"Do they at least donate the tree?"

"No."

"And you have to cover all the expenses?"

"It's for a good cause."

"And tell me again what you get out of this, besides two pairs of tickets to this charity gala?"

"I get to sponsor something worthwhile."

She worked so hard, and she sounded so excited. He worried about her pushing so hard and juggling so many things but he didn't want to dampen her enthusiasm. "I think it's awesome what you're doing."

"You do? Yay! I was worried you'd say something about me already having so much on my plate, and it is happening really soon, so it's going to be a push to get everything done, but I'll just work hard this weekend. You don't mind, do you?"

"Of course not. And it seems to me you like being busy. I don't think you'd know what to do with yourself if you didn't have a couple projects going on all at one time."

She laughed, amused. "So true. I'm not very good at relaxing."

Strangely, he understood. He'd never enjoyed doing nothing. It was why he got into real estate. "So what is the attire for party?"

"Dressy, but I'm not sure it's black tie. I'll have to look into that."

"I can clean up alright, but I don't have a tux."

"I don't think you need one. You're so fine you could probably walk in wearing just your Wranglers and an open flannel."

Rory laughed softly, appreciatively. She knew how to make him feel like a million bucks. "So when do I see you again?"

"Soon. Hopefully."

"Soon sounds good," he agreed. "Let's plan on dinner this weekend. Maybe I can make you dinner at my place Saturday night?"

"Can you cook?"

"I don't look like I'm starving, do I?"

"Uh, no. You look, um, perfect."

He grinned again, his body heating, hardening. He wanted her so much. She tested the limits of his self-control. "Dinner Saturday will make four dates. You do know what that means?"

"That you're still competitive with Paul?"

"He's not my rival."

"He's not your rival," she agreed. "Not even close." She hesitated, before adding, "Because you have no rival."

"No?"

"No." Her voice was breathless. She sounded impossibly sweet. "There's no one I like as much as you. There's no one else I want to be with, either. There is just you."

He was silent letting the words sink in. They sounded good and they felt even better. "You don't have to make any big decisions until date five."

Her light, tinkling laugh made him smile. She sounded so happy. It felt good to know he could make her happy. "We have a good thing here," he said. "And it's just going to keep getting better."

"I hope so."

"I know so," he answered firmly. "We can make this go the distance."

"How do you know?"

"Just a gut feeling."

Her cheeks turned pink. "And you have a good gut?"

"The best."

ON FRIDAY, IN between applying coats of paint and varnish to a headboard and coffee table, Sadie went through all the ornaments she'd collected since she was a girl. She'd always had a weakness for antique ornaments, and she'd bought boxes and boxes of over the years, picking up six at a flea market, and then a dozen in a second hand store, four in an antique store, and two dozen from eBay. Her collection was enormous, which meant she had more than enough of the delicate rose, blue, silver and gold balls and spheres to cover an eight foot Christmas tree. The glittering antique ornaments would look beautiful paired with the inexpensive clear glass balls she'd bought at a discount store two years ago, the clear glass reflecting the colors of the antique ornaments and the lights of the tree.

But by midafternoon she was missing Rory and she texted him to see if he could meet for coffee. He didn't answer right away. In fact, it was nearly an hour before she heard from him. *"Sorry. Have been at the airport and now heading to our old ranch in Paradise Valley. Are we still on for tomorrow?"*

"Yes," she texted back. *"Of course."*

THE BULL RIDER interested in the Douglas property was Chase Garrett, and he was interested in purchasing the ranch to work it with his brothers.

Rory had always liked Chase, and the offer that came in this morning was such a solid, respectable one, it made Rory admire Chase more.

While Rory liked the offer, he was uncomfortable accepting without someone coming out to have a look at the property and so this afternoon Rory picked up the Denver realtor from the Bozeman airport, and drove him out to the Douglas Ranch. They tramped around a bit, as they walked around, the sun came out from behind the clouds and splashed the landscape with golden light.

"Beautiful views from up here," the realtor said as Rory drove him up to the foothills.

"God's country," Rory answered quietly.

The realtor glanced at Rory. "Is it going to be hard to let this all go?"

"No. It's time."

Rory signed the offer sitting at a café in a strip mall not far from the Bozeman airport. He accepted all the terms and conditions. There was no need to make a counter offer. The offer was clean and strong and Rory understood that Chase wanted to close soon. Rory wanted to close, too, ready for new beginnings.

They were exiting the café and heading back to the truck when Rory spotted a large snow globe in the window of the gift shop next door. It was bigger than the traditional snow globe, with the glass resting on an ornate silver base. What caught his eye, though, was the shape of the mountain inside the globe. It looked like Copper Mountain with the same distinctive peak.

He stepped closer to the window for a better look. Three scenes had been cut into the mountain and he immediately thought of Sadie. In one scene a pair ice skated on a tiny frozen pond, while in another a couple rode in a horse drawn carriage, and then in the last, a couple strolled down a festive Victorian-looking street.

Rory felt as though he were looking at Marietta one hundred and twenty some years ago. It would have been around the time his great-great-grandfather, Sinclair Douglas, an Irish miner who'd come from Butte to work Copper Mountain purchased the land in Paradise Valley, and married McKenna Frasier, Paradise Valley's first schoolteacher.

And now Rory had just signed away the ranch Sin Douglas had purchased.

But it was time. Rory, Quinn, and McKenna needed to be free of the past. They needed a fresh start. And looking at the miniature scenes carved into the towering mountain, Rory was somehow certain his great-great-grandfather would approve. After all, Sin Douglas was a man who'd left Butte to start fresh, and by starting over, he'd achieved great things.

Rory was ready to achieve great things, even if those great things were as simple as getting married and becoming a father.

While the realtor made phone calls outside, Rory went into the gift shop and paid for the snow globe. And then with the oversized globe bubble wrapped and placed in a shopping bag, Rory returned to his truck and drove the realtor to the airport, and then finally headed back to Marietta.

It had been a long day, but a good day. A day of endings and new beginnings and a snow globe that made him smile.

It was only when he was close to his renovated stable-house that he realized he didn't want to wait to give Sadie the snow globe. He'd missed her today and he wanted to tell her about everything that had happened, and he didn't want to go to bed without seeing her beautiful face.

He called her as he approached Chance Avenue. She picked up right away.

"I have something for you," he said. "I'm on your way to your house now."

"You don't know where I live."

"You're on Chance Avenue, aren't you? Just go outside and wait for me. I'll find you."

Rory had avoided this street for years, and now he was on it, and he was glad, glad to be driving it today because today was about endings and new beginnings, and he was ready to move forward. He was finally making peace with his past and, just maybe, peace with himself.

He traveled three blocks before he saw her ahead. She was holding her phone, the light illuminating her face. She waved at him. He lifted a hand in acknowledgement as he slowed, braking in front of the house. But as he shifted into park, he did a double take recognizing the small house with its boxy shape, the picket fence where most people in the neighborhood had chain link fences, and the narrow sliver of a front yard dominated by the big tree in the front corner, significant because the tree's roots had cracked and buckled the sidewalk running past.

Rory slowly turned off the ignition, eyes narrowing. There was no way. She wasn't...

It had to be just a weird coincidence that Sadie was standing in front of the house where he'd dropped McKenna that night because Sadie couldn't be the girl... the one who'd had the party... could she?

What were the odds? It was improbable, impossible.

Stepping out of the truck, Rory pocketed his keys and tried to collect his thoughts.

"Hey." Sadie came towards him, smiling, and yet there was something a little anxious in her expression, a wariness in her eyes, and his gut knew that she'd been worried about this. She hadn't wanted him to come to her house. *Why?*

"So darlin'," he said slowly, trying to keep his temper in check, "want to fill me in on what's going on?"

"What do you mean?"

"This is the house. And you're the girl. The girl who apparently likes to keep secrets."

SADIE SHIVERED AT the hardness in his voice. His expression was just as flinty. He was angry.

"Can we go inside?" she said, "Talk there where it's warmer?"

"I need to get on the road."

She drew a careful breath, shoulders hunching against the cold. "I didn't know how to tell you. But then, I wasn't sure you'd remember, or care."

"Not remember?" he ground out, tone low and harsh and icy cold. "Not remember the day my family was murdered?"

She flinched. "I didn't mean it that way. I meant that a lot happened on that day, and I didn't know if my party mattered, or that I mattered."

"Mac was here when it happened."

"Yes."

"The only reason she survived was because she was here."

"Yes."

"How does that not matter?"

Sadie swallowed around the lump filling her throat. "I didn't mean that McKenna didn't matter, or that it wasn't important—" She broke off, air bottling in her lungs because she'd wondered all these years how Rory would react if he knew that she was the one who'd had the party, and it was her house that McKenna was at. And now she knew. And it wasn't good. She rubbed her hands together and then cupped them over her mouth, breathing on her fingers to warm them up. "I'm freezing, Rory. Please come into the house."

"No."

"At least let me get a coat."

"No need. I'm leaving."

Her eyes stung. "Don't go angry. *Please.*"

"Sadie, I don't know what to think right now."

"Think about what?"

"About you, this, all of us." He turned away, glanced down the dark street where the small houses lined up in an untidy row. She watched him scan the street and then look at his truck and then finally look back at her. "I don't get it," he said at length. "I don't get this game you've been playing."

Her heart lurched, her insides heaving. "There's been no game."

"You said you used to pray for me—"

"I did."

"And you followed my career."

"Yes."

"And you even came to see me, night after night. I always wondered why. Why me. I understand now."

"Understand *what*?"

"The guilt. Your emotions. How upset you've been. I finally get it, and I don't like it. I don't want to be a part of it. Let's not do this anymore."

"*Rory.*"

"Don't." His voice was rough, sharp, and it stopped her next words. "The truth is, you never desired me, and you certainly didn't love me. What you felt was pity and maybe some twisted fascination. I've met women like you. They don't want a normal relationship, and they don't want a healthy man. They want someone sick and broken because it makes them feel powerful."

Her stomach heaved again. She felt as if she was going to be sick. "You're wrong."

"Then why keep where you lived a secret? And you have. We both know you have. I've offered to pick you up our dates, and each time you had some excuse. Why didn't I see that before? My rental house is four blocks from here. It's maybe a seven minute walk. The fact that you didn't *want* me to come here speaks volumes."

"I just didn't want to stir up unhappy memories."

"And not bringing up that night is supposed to be better?"

"*Yes.* You hated Marietta. You never returned."

"You're right, and I hated this street, too, because every time I saw it, it reminded me of Mac's last day being a happy, normal girl. She was only thirteen. Still a kid. I dropped her off for a slumber party and she practically skipped up the front walk, and then the next time I saw her, a couple hours later, I had to tell her that Mom and Dad were dead, and oh, Gordon, Ty, and Grace, too."

Rory's fury made the night crackle and snap. Sadie couldn't stop shivering. Her teeth kept chattering. She wanted to tell him that she understood, far more then he knew, because it was her last night being a secure little girl, too. "That's why I didn't say anything. It's why I felt guilty. I've always wondered if you hadn't brought her here, would things have been different?"

"*Yes.* If she hadn't been here, she would have probably

died, too. She lived because she wasn't there. I lived because I was bringing her here. And I don't know why we both escaped the blood bath, but we did. And it was all because my folks asked me to drive her here, for your party."

Sadie blinked back tears. "I'm so sorry."

"I am, too." He gave his head a slight shake. "I need to go."

She wanted to ask him to please stay, just for a little longer. She wanted him to come in so she could explain why it was difficult for her to tell him about her party. She wanted him to take her in his arms and hold her and tell her everything would be okay. But she didn't think everything would be okay. She had the feeling that nothing would ever be the same between them again.

"Will you call me later?" she asked unsteadily.

"I don't know."

Sadie stood shivering on the sidewalk watching him drive away, her gaze pinned on the red tail lights until they disappeared from view.

CHAPTER ELEVEN

RORY DIDN'T KNOW where to go. He was angry, truly angry, the kind of anger that put him on the road, doing stupid things, making he want to drink too hard, and fight too much.

Impotent rage filled him now. He couldn't return to the little rental house. He didn't feel like going to Grey's—that was just asking for trouble. He didn't want to talk to anyone, much less anyone he knew. And so he got on Highway 89, and headed north to the 35 and then east for his ranch outside Clark.

It'd take him two and a half hours to reach Clark, and another thirty minutes to reach the house and his bed, and by then, Rory hoped he wouldn't feel like putting his fist through a wall or throwing bottles through a window.

This anger was why he rode bulls.

This anger was why he embraced danger.

And now he was furious, but this time it was at Sadie.

It took him all of three hours, but by the time he reached Wyoming, Rory had settled down. He wasn't angry anymore, just tired, and disappointed.

He didn't know why he'd gotten so upset so quickly—no, that wasn't true. He knew why. Chance Avenue had been a problem for him. Just like the Douglas Ranch had been a problem, and the cemetery, too.

Until a week ago, Rory didn't return to Marietta often, and when he did go back, it was for a day, and he avoided anyplace remotely uncomfortable, and all he'd done this past week was be uncomfortable.

He'd deliberately pushed himself out of his comfort zone, wanting to change for Sadie, wanting to be that man who could be in touch with his feelings, which meant opening up, and feeling, and growing, and letting go.

Clearly it was too much for a man who'd spent the past twenty something years choosing to be isolated, detached, and stunted.

Parking in front of the low log cabin, Rory lifted the bubble wrapped snow globe from the floor of the truck and carried it into the house with him. Even without peeling the wrap away, he could see the three scenes carved into the mountain, and he remembered how he'd felt when he found the snow globe.

He'd felt hope. And he'd felt love. And he couldn't wait to give it to Sadie.

He should have given it to her, too. He should have done what he'd intended to do when he went to her house. Instead he snapped and pushed her away. Hard.

There was no reason to be so rough. She didn't deserve

it. And it seemed despite all the growing up he'd tried to do lately, it wasn't enough.

SADIE WASN'T GOOD with conflict. Her mom hadn't been good with conflict, either, and had always struggled to stand up for herself. It was why her mother never asked for a raise, and continued to clean people's homes for the same price for almost fifteen years. When Sadie had tried to talk to her about asking her employers for more, citing the cost of living, and the fact that Mrs. Mann had an excellent work history, her mom always refused, saying she didn't want to create trouble. She wasn't comfortable making waves.

Lying in bed, unable to sleep after her confrontation with Rory, Sadie wished she'd learned how to handle conflict better. And uncomfortable conversations. Maybe then she could have just told Rory the things she'd wanted to tell him.

She thought if she'd found the right words he might understand why discussing the night of the tragedy with him was so difficult for her.

Because what happened at his home, happened on her birthday, her actual birthday, and the memories of that night were so upsetting that she'd never wanted another birthday party. And forever since, her birthday marked the anniversary of the deadly home invasion at the Douglas ranch.

It was as if she couldn't escape the past, or the violence.

She couldn't forget any of it, and instead of just worrying

about Rory, Quinn, and McKenna, she prayed for them, all of them but over time Rory was the one that stayed in her heart. Rory was the one she couldn't forget. The crazy thing was, she wanted to forget him. She wanted to meet someone wonderful and handsome, someone she could fall in love with so she never had to think about the violence again. She dated, though, and she tried to put herself out there, but she never met anyone who could replace Rory in her heart. It would have been so much easier if she had.

And so she'd accepted that he was supposed to be there, for whatever reason. But he wasn't the easiest of loves. He never had been.

RORY SPENT THE weekend trying to settle back into the routine of the ranch, the property tucked against the foothills of the Shoshone National Forest, the land so different here from Paradise Valley, which is why he'd bought it.

Thoughts of Sadie kept creeping in, even though he didn't want to think about her. But every time he wasn't riding, or hauling feed, or repairing machinery, he found himself picturing her on the street, shivering, as she looked at him with wide, frightened eyes.

At first he'd told himself it was part of her act—the worry, the confusion, the emotions—and then he hated himself for thinking that way because he didn't believe it was true. He didn't really believe she'd played him. He believed her when she said she didn't want to upset him by bringing up the past. Everyone felt that way about the tragedy on the ranch. It was a taboo topic. It only created pain.

So why had he been so angry with her? Why had he been so hard on her?

The answer came to him as he was inspecting the deicer for the horses' water trough. She'd caught him off guard, and he'd reacted badly because of that.

For Rory, control was everything. It was why he'd chosen to compete on the rodeo circuit, and then later, focus on riding broncs and bulls. It was dangerous, and demanding, and it required every ounce of his skill and concentration. Riding a massive, kicking, bucking animal tested his control, and there was no greater thrill—or relief—when he won. Every ride was a challenge, and every ride pushed him to his limits, and just being able to walk away after a wild, rough ride reassured him that he was still in control.

Maybe the problem with Sadie was that he cared so much, he wasn't in control.

But that wasn't her fault. That was his.

An hour later after returning to the house he sent her a text. *"We should talk."*

SADIE SAT BACK on her heels and gazed up at her handiwork. The tree was finished and it looked gorgeous. She was usually her own worst critic but she couldn't find fault with her tree and no one else in the Graff ballroom had anything like hers. Her theme "A Very Vintage Christmas", was inspired by her love of Marietta, and the Graff Hotel, and her beaded ornaments shimmered in between the gorgeous antique ornaments. Long strands of pearls draped the tree, and then to add some warmth and depth, she tucked a rich red velvet ribbon in and out of the branches so that the wide velvet just peeked out of the greenery adding a lovely softness to the crisp green boughs.

She hoped the tree would go to a high bidder. She hadn't been frugal at all but the tree had become her therapy as the days passed without a word from Rory.

McKenna said he'd left town, too, and Sadie was devastated. She'd always feared this would happen—that she'd begin to get comfortable with him and then he'd leave—but she wasn't going to crack today, and she wasn't going to take to her bed tonight.

No, she was going to the party and she'd be confident and radiant. While putting the finishing touches on the tree, she pictured the beautiful dress she'd found to wear tonight. It was slinky and form fitting, a gorgeous teal satin with exquisite beading, and she'd planned to wear her hair down, but add some glamorous waves around her face. McKenna and Trey were still going with her, and Sadie wasn't going to let them know how hurt she was that Rory had just disappeared from her life as if she didn't matter.

Gathering her empty ornament boxes, she stacked them

on the cart provided by the hotel, and was pushing the cart out of the ballroom and down the hotel corridor towards the back parking lot when she heard her phone vibrate. Sadie fished out her phone and checked for messages. A missed call from McKenna, and a text from Rory.

His text was brutally short and impersonal. *"We should talk."*

Her eyes stung and she blinked hard to keep them from filling with tears.

He was going to break things off with her, she was sure of it, after a message like that, and the pain was staggering. Her heart fell, tumbling straight to her feet. Still fighting tears, she pushed the cart across the parking lot, the wind gusting, threatening to send her cardboard boxes in every direction. She glanced up at the sky, the clouds were high but thickly banked. Snow.

Of course. It hadn't snowed in weeks and now, the night of the gala, it would snow. Hopefully it wouldn't be too bad. She quickly loaded the boxes into her trunk and then returned the cart to the hotel's catering department. And then, she finally replied to Rory's text, determined to be calm and keep it together. *"Can we talk tomorrow? Tonight is the tree auction and I'm running behind."*

Tomorrow would be better, she told herself. Whatever he wanted to say could wait. Tonight was her night. She was going to enjoy tonight no matter what.

Swallowing hard, blinking fiercely, Sadie walked back to

her car and the first thick white flakes slowly drifted down from the sky. *No,* she told herself, blinking again. *No, you will absolutely, positively not cry.*

THE AUCTION WAS tonight.

Rory couldn't believe he'd forgotten. Had that many days gone by already?

He called McKenna. She answered, but not very friendly. "What's the deal with you?"

"Tonight's the auction."

"Mistletoe and Montana, yes."

"Are you going?"

"Sadie invited us. We were supposed to be sitting with you two."

"I forgot it was tonight."

"But that's probably because you forgot about her."

"I didn't forget about her."

"So you just leave town and don't say a word?"

"I had to sort a few things out."

"Whatever. I'm not interested in details—"

"I'm coming tonight," he interrupted, shoving clothes in a bag as he talked. "I'm going to be there."

"There's a snow storm predicted for the pass. You can't drive it now."

"Should take me just about three hours if I leave now."

"Rory. Just call her, apologize, but don't drive tonight.

It's not safe."

"I'm heading to my truck. See you soon." He hung up and walked outside.

Snow was falling, fairly steadily, but it didn't trouble him. You couldn't grow up in Montana without dealing with some formidable winter conditions. He placed his bags in the back seat of the cab and then remembered the snow globe in the house. He returned for the snow globe and then climbed behind the steering wheel, setting off for Marietta.

Forty minutes later, the snow was coming down so hard Rory's windshield wipers couldn't keep up and the blinding wall of white meant he couldn't see tail lights around him.

Fortunately, he knew the road well, and he tried to stay relaxed, and alert, to be ready for anything unexpected.

If it weren't snowing so hard, he would have called Sadie to let her know he was on his way, but this was pretty much blizzard conditions and her dad had died in Wyoming during one of the infamous whiteouts, and the last thing Rory wanted to do was add to her worry.

The goal was to get there, and once there, he'd make amends. But until he reached Marietta, there was nothing he could do but let the stereo keep him company as the howling winds blew thick drifts of snow across the highway, turning the landscape into a blinding white. Snow now piled high in every direction, burying landmarks, and covering signposts.

It was slow going now, but he'd get there. Possibly late, but he would get there, and he would be her date.

An hour later he wasn't going anywhere.

Law enforcement closed the interstate down outside Billings, with highway patrol cars lined on both sides of the freeway, forming a blockade, their blue lights flashing.

Rory felt sick as he sat, trapped in the truck, unable to move. Time was passing and the event would have started by now and he pictured Sadie there with McKenna and Trey. He pictured his place at the table, empty. His place shouldn't be empty. He should have been there. He should have remembered that the auction was today. He should have not left town in a temper, either.

He had to make this right. But to do that, he needed the snow to stop, and the freeway to reopen, and both things could happen, if the stars aligned right.

But an hour crawled by with the snow continued to fall, and the wind howled, sending huge sheets of white blowing across the freeway.

It's just a re-ride, Rory told himself, and he'd had countless re-rides during his career. The storm could blow out, and the roads could be plowed and he could be heading on to Marietta in no time.

He wouldn't get discouraged. He wouldn't give up. He was going to get there.

But another hour passed, and the time slid away, eight o'clock becoming nine, and nine becoming nine thirty, he was forced to accept it wasn't going to happen. Because even if the roads opened now, it was still another ninety minutes to Marietta, and the event wouldn't last all night. Once the trees were auctioned, people would leave. Sadie would leave.

Rory texted McKenna. *"It doesn't look good."*

She texted back. *"I figured as much. Everyone's talking about the storm."*

"How is it there? Hard snow?"

"Not as bad as Billings."

"That's where I'm now."

"Sadie's tree is up next."

Rory's chest ached. *"How does it look?"*

"Gorgeous."

"Buy it for me. Just don't let her know I'm bidding."

"I'll have Taylor do it. Where do you want it delivered tomorrow?"

"Sadie's house."

And then fifteen minutes later he got another text. *"It's yours, and it only cost you an arm and a leg."*

He answered with an emoji of a smiley face.

She answered with an emoji blowing a kiss.

Rory started to put away his phone and then he pulled it back out and sent Sadie a text. *"I am truly sorry to miss the party. I've been thinking of you all night."* And then he put the phone back, and turned the radio up as he heard Jennifer Nettles song "Count Your Blessings Instead of Sheep" come on.

He felt as though he'd swallowed a bucket of nails as he listened to the lyrics and he gripped the steering wheel, feeling like a failure. He hated letting Sadie down. He'd wanted to be the man she needed, the man with integrity, the man who'd do the right thing.

He hadn't done the right thing by walking away from her the other night, and he vowed then and there, that if she gave him another chance, it'd never happen again.

If he had the chance...

The chance. A chance.

He suddenly flashed back to that night in Clovis, and his prayer. *Lord, give me a chance.* Maybe it was being trapped on a freeway for five hours, buffeted by wind and blinding snow, but suddenly the prayer took on an entirely new meaning.

He'd prayed for help and a chance.

He'd prayed because he was in trouble.

He'd prayed because his mystery girl was there that night and he desperately wanted a chance with her.

And his prayer had been answered. Of course his prayer had been answered. And of course his girl would live on Chance Avenue, because where else did angel girls live?

Rory offered up a silent thank-you, and repeating his vow that he'd do better, he would.

A half hour later the road opened and Rory was driving. He'd missed the fundraiser at the Graff but he wasn't going to miss saying goodnight to Sadie.

SADIE LET HERSELF into her house, and hung up her heavy wool jacket with the faux fur trim in the hall closet before slipping her high heels off.

She took off one dangly sparkly earring and then the other. Barefoot, she walked around the house, the satin fabric of her gown sliding across her legs as she moved around the house, plugging in the tiny table top tree she'd placed on an end table in the living room, and then turning on music, letting the old fashioned Christmas carols fill the house with sound.

She wasn't going to think of Rory.

She wasn't going to be sad.

Yes, he'd sent that text during the auction—he was thinking of her—but if he was really thinking of her, he wouldn't be sending texts, he'd be there.

If he really cared, he wouldn't have blown her off tonight.

If he really cared—

She broke off, hot tears stinging her eyes; not wanting to think about him tonight because it'd just make her sad and she didn't want to be sad on such a spectacular evening. Her tree had been magnificent, drawing lots of attention. She'd been so gratified by everyone's response, and even more pleased by the money her tree had raised. The bidding had been fierce. She'd already been asked to participate in the tree auction next year, too, and a dozen others had asked her for business cards, wanting to know more about her business.

If people didn't know about Montana Rose before, they did now.

RORY ARRIVED AT Sadie's house on Chance Avenue at eleven thirty. Fresh snow covered the roof and sidewalk, and a light snow continued to fall.

As he parked his truck, he saw a shadow pass the living room window and lights come on, the snug living room glowing red, green, blue, and gold.

Standing on the sidewalk in front of her house he flashed back to the past, but this time it wasn't McKenna he saw running up the front walk. Instead he saw a little girl with bright copper hair waiting on the front porch for her guests to arrive. He imagined how excited she was to have everyone coming. Thirteen was a big deal. Sadie would have felt so grown up. She'd be feeling special and beautiful... finally a teenager.

A hard knot formed in his gut, the knot similar to the lump in his throat as he realized that her special night was ruined, too, and she'd done nothing wrong, but of course she'd felt guilty, and responsible, because that was what people did. They blamed themselves for being mortal, blamed themselves for not being god.

There was nothing she could have done.

Nothing at all.

The truth was, there was nothing any of them could have

done about that night. That's why it was a tragedy.

Drawing a breath Rory headed up the walk and rang the doorbell.

SADIE KNEW IT was him even before she'd peeked through the peephole, and her heart beat double-time when she saw his hat on the other side of the door, and his face in profile.

She opened the door, pulse thudding, breath catching, afraid of what he was here to say, but more afraid of not listening. Despite everything, she felt connected to him. Despite everything, he was still the one for her.

But did he feel the same way? Had he changed his mind?

"Hi," she whispered.

His gaze slid over her, from her carefully styled hair, down her slim fitting dress to her bare feet below.

"You look beautiful."

"You should have seen the earrings. They were something else."

"I screwed up, angel. I'm sorry."

Her lips parted, his apology catching her off guard. "It's—" She stropped, swallowed, eyes stinging. "You—" She stopped again, and then she lifted her chin and looked him in the eye. "You hurt me. Badly."

"I was wrong."

"It took you days to reach out to me. *Five* days."

"Way too long."

"You should have said something sooner."

"I should have apologized as soon as I understood why I was upset. I'm sorry. I'll do better. I promise."

"Come in. It's freezing out there."

He stepped inside, snowflakes clinging to his hat and coat. "I tried to make it tonight," he said. "They closed the interstate at Billings."

"You shouldn't have tried driving tonight—"

"I wanted to be with you."

"Then you should have been here this morning. Better yet, you shouldn't have left at all."

"I agree."

He just stood there looking lost in her entry and it made her heart feel funny. "Give me your coat."

"You're sure?"

"Yes." She hung up his winter coat in her closet and watched as he took off his hat, placing it on her small hall table.

"How long did it take you to get back?" she asked.

"I left Clark around four."

She looked at the clock on the living room mantle. It was nearly midnight now. "You've been driving that entire time?"

He nodded.

"You must be exhausted."

"It's nothing."

And yet she could tell from his face, and the white lines at his eyes and the deep grooves at his mouth that it was something. "Are you hungry?"

"I'm fine. Really. Don't worry about me."

"Something's going on, though. I can see it in your face."

"I'm mad," he said shortly. "Mad at myself. I don't want to lose you, darlin'. I can't lose you. I love you."

"You can't, not if you think I'm demented—"

"I never said you were demented. I said I'd met women who didn't want a healthy man, but I didn't mean it about you."

"Why did you say it then?"

"I was angry, and was caught off guard, so I do what a man like me does when things feel out of control. I fight. I defend myself. And that's what I did." He shook his head. "I'm not proud of it, Sadie. I don't feel good about any of this. And it's not an excuse, but the reason I was so... off guard... was because this was about the ranch, and what happened that night. I normally don't lose it like that. This just happened to be where I was particularly... weak."

She was tired of all the words. Truthfully, she wasn't angry anymore and she didn't want to talk. She just wanted him to hug her, and hold her, and make her feel safe again. "I'm sorry, too. I'm sorry I didn't tell you who I was earlier. I wasn't sure how to work it into the conversation... it always felt weird and awkward trying to say that it was my house you dropped McKenna off at, because it felt like I was making the... thing... about me, when it wasn't about me at all."

"And yet it was about you. It was your night, and your night was hijacked about something horrible."

Tears filled her eyes and her lower lip trembled. "Let's not talk about it anymore."

"No, let's. Because this has been a something between us for all these years, and it's not necessarily an awful thing. It ties us together."

"Then I need something warmer to wear and a cup of tea."

"I'll put the water on. You go change."

She met him in the kitchen just a few minutes later, grateful to be out of her slinky gown and into warm pajamas topped with a fleecy sweatshirt. The kettle was coming to a boil as she entered and she felt a little pang as she saw he'd found her Christmas mugs and had them out on the counter with a teabag in each.

"Look at you," she said.

"I have my uses," he answered, filling the cups with hot water and then carrying them to the small kitchen table.

She sat down and pulled her cup closer and felt another pang as she realized he'd chosen mint tea. Her favorite tea for evenings. Her eyes burned all over again and her heart felt impossibly tender. "We're going to be okay, right?"

"You and me?" he clarified, pulling out the chair opposite hers and sitting down. "Yeah. We are, babe."

"Then why do we have to talk about the past?"

"Because the past is a big part of us, and if we want a future, I think we've got to clear up some of the confusion, and set the record straight, once and for all."

"I don't even know where to start."

"Start with you party. Tell me about it."

Sadie slowly exhaled, trying to find the words, wanting to get it right. "It was a big deal for me. It was the biggest night of my life. I know that might sound silly, but I'd never had a sleepover, and just days before it happened it looked like no one was coming and then McKenna's cheer competition got changed and she called to say she could come, and then suddenly all the other girls were coming, too." She nodded, eyes scratchy. "You have no idea how excited I was that McKenna could come. She was so popular and yet she was also really kind to me. No one popular had ever been that nice."

"Don't say that."

"But it's true." She turned her cup a little, positioning the handle close to her hand. "You don't know how things like that can make a difference. My mom wasn't a mom that played bridge or bunco. She didn't get her hair professionally done. She didn't wear stylish clothes. She was a maid. She scrubbed toilets for the families that could afford to hire help, and families that could afford help didn't want their daughters hanging out here, on Chance Avenue, and I certainly wasn't going to be invited to their big nice house. So having a party, and an opportunity to show people who I was, was huge."

He said nothing. His head was down, his gaze focused on the steam rising from his cup but she could tell her was listening intently.

Heart pounding, Sadie forced herself to continue. "I was standing on the front porch when you dropped her off, and then I watched you pull away."

"You remember that day?"

"I remember every little detail." She struggled to smile but failed. "I remember her arriving with her sleeping bag and the present. I remember you leaving, and how you accelerated fast. Your window was down and your music was loud and you looked all golden from the sunlight." She took a shuddering breath as her throat began to seal closed. "And then I remember the sheriffs coming and collecting McKenna to take to the hospital."

Still he said nothing.

She reached up and wiped away a tear, and then another. "And maybe I could have put it in the past, but every year on my birthday I think of your family, and I think of McKenna, and I think of you and how you looked that day, leaving here. You were so handsome and so... perfect... and I think about how just thirty minutes later you... found what you found and it breaks my heart. Still." The tears were falling so fast she couldn't stop them. "I hate what happened to you, Rory. I hate that you had to be the one to find them all—"

"But if it hadn't been me, Quinn would have died." Rory looked at her now, his eyes pink from tears he fought to suppress. "If I'd stopped anywhere, or hadn't driven fast, he would have been gone before I got back. So I'm grateful it was me. It gave him a chance."

And then suddenly his jaw tightened and tears welled in his eyes and he looked away, unable to let her see him cry.

"I have to tell you something, Sadie," he said, his voice low and hoarse. "I've never told anyone this, but every night before I compete, I pray. For years I have prayed nightly for McKenna and Quinn. I have never asked God for anything for me, and then that night in Clovis, the night you were there this last August, I knew I was in trouble as Hammerfall threw his head back and I went flying forward. I knew in that split second it was bad. Really bad. And I prayed as I flew forward. I asked God to give me a chance."

Sadie stared at him, her fist pressed to her mouth.

"Darlin', I wouldn't have prayed if you hadn't been there. But for some reason I did that night, and I wasn't asking Him to let me live. I was asking to live so I could have a chance with you. God heard me that night. He saved me, for you, my angel girl."

She shook her head.

"Yes. He saved me so that I could make sure you have the best life possible, and I know we've had bumps, and I expect we'll have more, because life isn't always going to be smooth, but I'm here because I love you, and I want to be together with you. I want to marry you, and have those babies with you. I want to be your man... if you'd give me a

202

chance."

"You are the only one I've ever loved, Rory."

He stood up and came around the table, drawing her to her feet, and then his arms were around her, and he was holding her, just as she'd needed to be held. "I love you, Sadie, and there is no doubt in my mind that we're meant to be together, forever."

She gave him a tremulous smile. "Forever, and a day."

The corner of his mouth curved. "Marry me, darlin'. Let's have those babies together."

"Yes," she whispered, "But…"

His eyebrow lifted. "But?"

"Maybe we should sit back down for this," she murmured.

He sat down and then drew her onto his lap. "What's happened?"

"Nothing. But, um… you know I want children."

"Badly."

"Yes, but I've been thinking, would it be okay if we didn't rush into the baby thing? Would it be okay if you and I just had a year, or two, to ourselves?" She lightly stroked his brow and then the high hard line of his cheekbone. "I feel like I can't ever get enough time with you and maybe it's selfish, but I'd really like a year, or two, where it's just us, before I have to start sharing you with anybody else."

He looked into her eyes intently, and then slowly smiled. "I can do that."

"You're sure?"

"Absolutely." He kissed her, and then again. "But we can practice the baby making, right? Just to be sure we know what we're doing."

She smiled against his mouth. "That's probably wise."

She could feel him smile back, and then she kissed him, loving him, so very, very much. "You feel like Christmas, Rory Douglas."

"And you feel like hope." He drew back to study her and smooth her long hair back from her face. "To think I found my miracle on Chance Avenue."

"Where else would a miracle be?"

He grinned, fingertips tracing the curve of her cheek and the corner of her lips. "What would I do without you?"

"Good thing you don't have to worry about it. I've been crazy about you since I was a girl. I think you're pretty much stuck with you." *me*

"Perfect."

"I love you, Rory."

"And I love you, angel heart."

Epilogue

Two years later

"RORY, BABE, YOU can't keep buying my tree at the auction," Sadie said, part exasperated, part amused, as they stood on the front porch watching the delivery truck try to position itself near their driveway on Bramble. Normally it wouldn't be a problem but there had been a massive snowstorm two days before and the roads were still lined with huge piles cleared by the snow plow.

"Why not? I love your trees. I want your trees, especially after I see all the work you put into them," he answered, shifting the nine month old in his arms, trying to keep the baby from wiggling out of the blanket he'd thrown around him. "You want mama's tree here, too, don't you, bud?" he added to the baby.

"Yes, to create as much havoc as possible." She laughed, leaning towards her guys, and giving Rory a kiss, and then Kelly, and just like that, the babe inside her gave a lusty kick. She put a hand to her round belly, and patted it. "This one is dying to get in on the action."

"Kicking again?" Rory asked, looking inordinately

pleased.

"You're smiling because it's not your ribs he's kicking—"

"You keep saying he, darlin'. Do you know something you're not telling me?"

"No. But I can't keep calling the new baby 'it'. Makes me feel like I'm carrying an alien, instead of an angel."

Rory laughed, the warm, rich sound delighting Sadie as always. "I better go help that poor guy if we want to get your tree in the house in one piece."

"And we're going to go inside where it's warm."

Rory kissed her and handed over Kelly and she went into the house to watch from the large living room window, excited to be celebrating Christmas in their lovely home for the second year.

The past two years had been the best, happiest, most wonderful years. They'd also been incredibly busy. After a Christmas wedding two years ago, they'd spent several months traveling, visiting Hawaii, Fiji, then Australia where they saw some of Rory's bull rider friends, before returning to Marietta to look for a new place. They purchased an older house on Bramble in need of work. It wasn't grand, but with the right love, it could be a beautiful home, and while Rory tackled the structural issues with contractors, Sadie tackled the interior. It took months to get it ready, and they moved in just in time for their first Thanksgiving.

It must have been somewhere between Thanksgiving and Christmas they conceived Kelly, and now, there was another little Douglas on the way, and Sadie felt beyond blessed.

Kelly suddenly spotted Rory coming up the walkway with the tree, and he squealed with delight.

Sadie laughed at his exuberance. "You do love your Da-da," she said, kissing his still very bald head. The family was taking bets on his hair color—if and when it finally grew in. McKenna said Kelly would be a blonde like Rory. Rory thought his first born would be red like his mom and Aunt McKenna. And Sadie didn't care. She was actually hoping it didn't grow in too fast because a baby's bald head demanded endless kisses.

Kelly looked up at her, and laughing, tried to squeeze his hand into her mouth. "No."

He laughed harder, and tried again.

"You're a very persistent Douglas," she said with mock severity, because she loved that trait about him.

In fact, she loved everything about her beautiful, joyful life with Rory. It was so hard to believe that just two years ago she'd given Rory up, and yet here they were, in their own comfortable, warm home on lovely Bramble, with a healthy son, and another baby on the way, due to arrive late January, provided this one stayed put full term.

The smell of fragrant pine, and the swish of branches and the clink and tinkle of ornaments heralded the arrival of the tree into the house. Inexplicably, tears filled Sadie's eyes.

What an amazing, incredible miracle it all was. Life, love, and this ridiculous happiness she'd found with Rory.

Rory slipped the deliveryman a folded bill and then, turning to Sadie, he saw her tears.

"What's wrong?" he crossed quickly to her side. "Is your back bothering you again?"

"No." Smiling unsteadily, she knocked away the tears. "These are happy tears."

"You're sure?"

"Positive. I'm so grateful, and so blessed. Rory, you were my dream. How much luckier can one girl be?"

"I might be your dream, but you're still my miracle. And I thank the good Lord for you every single day. Merry almost Christmas, angel girl," he said, kissing her.

"Merry Christmas, baby, and you were absolutely worth the wait!"

THE END

LOVE ON CHANCE AVENUE SERIES

Book 1: *Take Me, Cowboy*
Winner of the RITA® Award for Best Romance Novella

Book 2: *Miracle on Chance Avenue*
View the series here!

Available now at your favorite online retailer!

Find out more about Rory's sister, McKenna Douglas, in
The Kidnapped Christmas Bride!

The Taming of the Sheenans

The Sheenans are six powerful wealthy brothers from
Marietta, Montana. They are big, tough, rugged men, and as
different as the Montana landscape.

Christmas at Copper Mountain
Book 1: Brock Sheenan's story

Tycoon's Kiss
Book 2: Troy Sheenan's story

The Kidnapped Christmas Bride
Book 3: Trey Sheenan's story

Taming of the Bachelor
Book 4: Dillion Sheenan's story

A Christmas Miracle for Daisy
Book 5: Cormac Sheenan's story

The Lost Sheenan's Bride
Book 6: Shane Sheenan's story

Available now at your favorite online retailer!

ABOUT THE AUTHOR

New York Times and USA Today bestselling author of over fifty five romances and women's fiction titles, **Jane Porter** has been a finalist for the prestigious RITA award five times and won in 2014 for Best Novella with her story, Take Me, Cowboy, from Tule Publishing. Today, Jane has over 12 million copies in print, including her wildly successful, Flirting With Forty, picked by Redbook as its Red Hot Summer Read, and reprinted six times in seven weeks before being made into a Lifetime movie starring Heather Locklear. A mother of three sons, Jane holds an MA in Writing from the University of San Francisco and makes her home in sunny San Clemente, CA with her surfer husband and two dogs.

Thank you for reading

Miracle on Chance Avenue

If you enjoyed this book, you can find more from all our great authors at TulePublishing.com, or from your favorite online retailer.

TULE
PUBLISHING